Alison Fell was born in Dumfries, [illegible] villages in the Highlands and Borders. She has published three novels, *Every Move You Make*, *The Black Box* and *Mer de Glace*. Her collection of poetry *Kisses for Mayakovsky* won the 1984 Alice Hunt Bartlett award. She lives in North London.

SERIOUS HYSTERICS

EDITED BY

Alison Fell

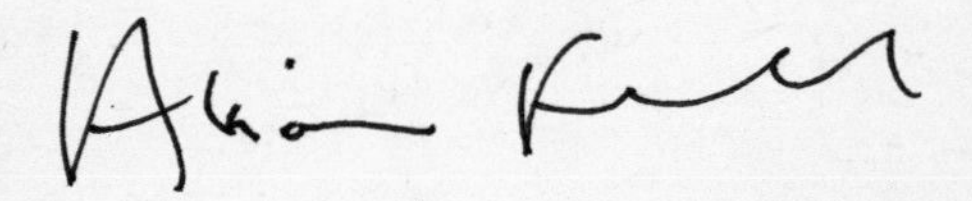

With thanks to Marsha Rowe, who originally suggested the idea of a book on hysteria.

The publishers thank Kathy Acker, Mark Ainley, Martin Chalmers, Mike Hart, John Kraniauskas, Bob Lumley, Enrico Palandri, Kate Pullinger for their advice and assistance

Library of Congress Catalog Card Number: 91-67840

British Library Cataloguing in Publication Data
Serious Hysterics
 I. Fell, Alison
 823[F]

 ISBN 1-85242-222-X

First published 1992 by
Serpent's Tail, 4 Blackstock Mews, London N4 and
401 West Broadway #2, New York, NY 10012

Typeset in 11/13½ pt. Ehrhardt by Setrite Typesetters, Hong Kong
Printed in Great Britain by Cox & Wyman Ltd., of Reading, Berkshire

CONTENTS

'When his patients came into possession of their own stories, Freud believed, they would not have to speak across the body. Yet Freud neglected to ask how a woman comes into possession of her own story, becomes a subject, when even narrative convention assigns her the place of an object of desire.'

Claire Kahane — *In Dora's Case*

'It is indeed true that one is ill when not loved; this means that a psychic structure that lacks an identifying metaphor or idealisation tends to realise it in that embodied non-object called somatic symptom — illness.'

Julia Kristeva — *Tales of Love*

'The sorrow that has no vent in tears makes other organs weep.'

Henry Maudsley, 19th C. anatomist

'By writing her self, woman will return to the body which has been more than confiscated from her, which has been turned into the uncanny stranger on display — the ailing or dead figure, which so often turns out to be the nasty companion, the cause and location of inhibitions. Censor the body and you censor breath and speech at the same time.'

Hélène Cixous — *La Jeune Née*

INTRODUCTION

In the long history of hysteria the Egyptians were the first to propose that the flight of the uterus from its normal position was the root cause of female disorders. It was a theory later taken up and elaborated by the Greeks, who gave the condition its name, after *husterikos*: uterus. 'The womb is an animal which longs to generate children,' wrote Plato, in a moving plea for the distressed organ; like Hippocrates, his recommendation to sufferers was marriage and pregnancy: in other words, a speedy submission to the patriarchal yoke.

Definitions of hysteria change radically down the centuries, but always the central theme of female deviance remains, and in all its manifestations the restless and migratory womb hovers like a dark eminence — the triangular uterus like the head of the devil, flanked by the two horns of the fallopian tubes — fascinating, alarming, disrupting the discourses of men.

In medieval times superstition replaced diagnostics, and symptoms like paralysis, partial anaesthesia, speech disorders and volatile emotional behaviour were all too easily ascribed to possession by the devil. Medical probing gave way to prodding with needles, to trussing and ducking and burning.

Freud himself saw a parallel between what was described in the *Malleus Maleficarum* and what he observed in the women patients he was treating. 'You remember having heard me say that the medieval theory of possession, upheld by the ecclesiastical tribunals, was identical to our theory of the foreign body and the splitting of consciousness,' he wrote to his friend Fliess in 1897. 'Why,' he went on to wonder, 'do the confessions extracted under torture have so much similarity to my patients' narratives during psychological treatment?'

In the ritual of exorcism women's bodies were bound so that the constraints would force the rampant demons out: the beastly symptom was set free, while the woman, purified, remained. The Greeks had used foul-smelling potions to drive the aberrant womb back to its proper place; later there were the bindings and the burnings, and later still in the theatre of catharsis came the purgatives, emetics. French feminist Catherine Clement makes a persuasive parallel between the spectacle of exorcism – 'I had a fantastic desire to see with my own eyes the sorceresses' rapture and their consorting with demons,' says Jean Boudin, inquisitor – and the famous *leçons du mardi* at the Salpêtrière Hospital in the 1880s, where Charcot put his troupe of hysterics through their paces for the edification of a mostly male audience.

Current definitions of hysteria make a distinction between hysteria as 'personality disorder' – characterised by a kind of excitable, attention-seeking behaviour which reads almost like a parody of femininity – and 'conversion hysteria', a form of the disease brought to a point of high art in the Victorian era. The middle class women observed by Freud transformed their repressed anger and desire into physical symptoms that simultaneously acknowledged and disowned the forbidden feelings. Memories, fantasies, feelings that could not flow, spoke instead across the body, borrowed organs and made them metaphors which could stand in for the scandalous contents of hearts and minds. Encouraged by Breuer's success with the patient Anna O., Freud began to use hypnosis to develop the 'talking cure' in which conversion symptoms such as paralysis, blindness, mutism and multilingualism were translated back into the narrative of their origin. Catharsis gives way, then, to psychoanalysis, humane in its quest to shine light on the Dark Ages of the unconscious and liberate the hysterics from their bonds.

Although far more benign than earlier exorcisms, when psychoanalysis sets out to invent itself, its terms, its patients, it too starts, inevitably, from phallocentric premisses. Filtering Dora through his own assumptions, desires and unconscious identifications, Freud becomes novelist and writes this famous story of hers, this classic narrative constructed from the counter-transference. Dora argues, struggles, but it's useless – the author has already decided on his story-line and is entranced by it. Dora writes the ending, though – by leaving, by giving the Herr Doktor his cards – and years later she's still vengeful. 'If there were any justice in the world, women would make laws and men would make babies,' she protests, laying herself open to all sorts of accusations – of ball-breaking, penis-envying, a whole new terminology ranged against her.

War still rages in feminist and psychoanalytical circles about Freud and his Dora story – a debate which is conducted in theoretical terms but which is above all a contest over authorship. Those of us who are writers, however, are less likely to seek scientific principles in the workings of the unconscious, more inclined to make poetry and mayhem from them. And if Freud's hobbled, partial, speechless women fascinate us still, we don't look on them as specimens. We are, after all, implicated. Locked in the symptoms lie the stories, the hidden pasts, the narratives of women — and also the question: how shall we exhibit what falls outside of patriarchal discourse? Added to this is the nagging suspicion that, far from being a dead duck, the repressive conservatism which forced Victorian women to frame their discontents in the code of the body is alive and well and living in Britain.

Female dis-order continues, then: the body as theatre, poet, storyteller; the unconscious demanding a hearing. The unconscious plays jokes, throws out warnings, messages, will always catch us out. We know what we do not know. A not-so-comical example: on the day I began my story — about hysterical blindness — I stuck a mascara brush in my eye, and after a painful half-blind week ended up at Moorfields Eye Hospital, where a 'foreign body' was removed under anaesthetic. And again: 'Blind' instinct had dictated that my heroine — a film-maker — be called Thea; only after I'd finished the story did I discover by chance the Greek derivation *theoros* — spectator, *thea* — a viewing.

And so to the characters in these stories, bedevilled (like the authors?) by symptoms. They are struck blind, grow lumps in the throat, suffer outbreaks of blisters, colitis. Some strike hysterical attitudes, others follow their wandering wombs to the point of crime; all operate within patriarchal discourse and none make their peace with it. Amy in Marsha's Rowe's 'Spinal Chords' wonders why her skin erupts in herpes bumps. Her intuition speaks across her body, trying to bring to light what she both knows and doesn't know — that her husband is being unfaithful. In Zoë Fairbairns's story young Elizabeth, like Freud's Dora, is forced to swallow both the lies and subterfuges of her father and the defensive denials of her mother — a baneful mix which literally sticks in her throat.

In Leslie Dick's 'Dysplasia' medical technology allows Gina to be a spectator at the theatre of her own symptoms. As doctors video her aberrant cervix, Gina speculates on the body perfect and imperfect, and how birth, death and the mother-daughter relationship are mediated by this transfixing medical discourse. In my own story, Thea the film director makes it in a man's world – and a Nazi one at that. Shored up by refusal, Thea 'simply can't see' why her friend Lilli sacrificed herself to save Jewish children. Years later, however, an attack of blindness acknowledges not only the feminine self which she has denied, but also her real betrayal of Lilli.

French theorist Luce Iragaray writes that '. . . the hysteric mimes her own sexuality in a masculine mode, since this is the only way she can rescue something of her own desire.' Set in Quebec, Gail Scott's story takes up this theme of woman-as-mimic and extends it into language itself. Living in a country split between the dominant discourse of English and the historically suppressed and less acceptable French, the elusive and kaleidoscopic S. muffles her mother tongue and adopts English as yet another mask with which to deflect her lover's pleas for intimacy.

In 'To Find Words' Lynne Tillman wittily applies the notion of hysterical splitting to the act of writing. 'Paige Turner,' a writer in search of a narrative, chases the lost and vital scene which might make the story complete. Meanwhile she is teased, prompted and manipulated by a phantom Voice which, exiled and unacknowledged, manifests itself in a persistent cough.

Since Hippocrates's time motherhood has been seen not only as woman's glory and destiny but also as the best possible cure for hysteria – a view fervently subscribed to by the convent-reared heroine of 'Be My Baby'. In Marina

Warner's poignant story of child-stealing the scornful and paranoid Norma blots out a past in which she has neglected her own children and creates instead an imaginary family which she elevates to the realms of the Holy. Nicole Ward Jouve focuses on a real family and its conflicts in 'Belly Cry'. As a girl, Anna represses her 'hysterical' fears and tries hard to be the good daughter, the brave daughter. Later, in the rôle of good wife, Anna must contain the strife and unspoken dreads of her parents, brother, husband, son. Her rebellious belly, however, spasmodic, refuses to contain anything.

From the symptoms, then, the stories spill out and spread: the clandestine biographies, our female narratives of dis-ease. The 'Phallocentric Performing Theatre' with its spectacular exorcisms faces closure, now that the foreign body has become our own, now that the flesh, turning its back on its audience, makes words . . .

Alison Fell

SPINAL CHORDS

Marsha Rowe

If hysteria is the feminine voice, that found its shape in the first one hundred years of the novel, it is also the voice that has no sound, no shape, that has been expressed only through the contortions of the body, the twists of the spine, the back that is too arched, the shoulders held stiffly, the leg, one or other of them, bent like a ballet dancer's too far to the outside or, pigeontoed, too far inwards. Such a voice is at the end of many generations of silence and of distortions.

It was two nights before Christmas Eve. Although Amy thought that Tom would probably wake from his nap in time to fetch their daughter Matilda from her friend's birthday party – Tom was reliable except for little things, like forgetting stuff from the supermarket – she kept her eye on the clock as she wrapped presents destined for Matilda's stocking. She felt round the sticky tape for the end, cut off a piece, stuck it on the paper wrapped round a wooden cat, dropped it into the bag. One down, still too many to go, scattered round her on the carpet. She must go down to the kitchen. Matilda always came home hungry from children's parties, despite stuffing herself with crisps, sweets, cake, all the food Amy had never cared for herself as a child. Party food.

She arched her back, stretched, reached for the trick money box feeling stiff and uncomfortable. She had herpes, at the top of her left buttock, just at the bottom of her spine, and it was aching. Earlier in the week she'd felt a burning irritation on the way home from a Christmas party. Lulled by wine, grappling with the hot mince pie the hostess insisted on giving them, she took no notice. The next morning, twisting in front of the mirror in the shower room, there was a small red lump and an angry red patch. The spot was tender, painful. She'd dosed herself with Rhus Tox until she was dizzy and smeared the spot with Calendula cream. No point visiting the doctor. From past experience she knew that the infection would take its course whatever she tried. What had made her ill? Working three weekends in a row? Surely not.

There had been, though, Tuesday. Crossing the road at the back of Marks & Spencer in Great Marlborough Street, she walked out from behind a parked van. She saw nothing, only heard the screech of brakes, then the horn. She ran blindly, noticing the shocked expression of the driver as she scuttled in front of him onto the pavement, her heart beating. She walked up the Marks & Spencer's steps, entered, looked at black opaque tights asking herself if they were the right sort of present for her eighteen-year-old niece and then, putting her hand to her heart under her yellow coat, realised that she'd walked in front of an oncoming car and nearly killed herself. What on earth was going on?

Standing in the aisle of tights, she suddenly remembered that this had happened before, when she was a child. She'd stood waiting to cross the road outside Neutral Bay Infants

School, Sydney, beside Mrs Evans, the mother of the two boys next door, who'd driven them all to school, and then she walked out onto the road just as a truck was looming over the hill. The truck had, unavoidably, nicked her. She'd fallen, just short of the front wheel.

Amy, walking away from the tights and heading upstairs, remembered how shaken and apologetic the driver had been. Poor man. It hadn't been his fault. Why had she done it? Seven years old. Nothing to do with her now. Mrs Evans had driven her back home where she had stayed in the flat with her mother for the rest of the day, bruised and shaken, aware of some indefinable longing. She steered her mind back to shopping, found a Marks & Spencer white cotton t-shirt, extra large, paid for it, moved on into women's underwear.

Sydney's pavements are slit across from inner to outer edge so the concrete can expand in the hot weather. Earth tremors, drought, extreme heat, crack the cement into crazy patterns. Weeds and grass grow up through the cracks. Occasionally the cement blocks buckle and twist indecently. Jumping the cracks is perilous. Amy does it at a run, school satchel thumping between her shoulders, silently reciting, if you land on a crack you'll break your mother's back, enjoying the force of her lithe young body running pell mell down the hill, accelerating, satchel thumping, bending knees, soles pounding, heels landing, get home, keep on. Breathless. Running.

Maps of Sydney show roads, houses, factories, offices, hospitals, schools, side streets, main streets, dead ends, parks, reserves, pools, not pavements. Trees are not on maps. Particularly not the trees Amy knows well. The enormous sinews of the Moreton Bay fig, rising up from the rocks behind Amy's flat, their roots descending from dark, lowering branches into the earth between crumbling sandstone. Nor the cracked elephant trunk of the peppercorn by the back fence. Nor the branches of the willow shredded every summer by clutching hands swinging out over the gulley. Nor the broad girth of the flame tree with its red beaking flowerets next to the swing. Not a single tree, not a single pavement.

The trees that lurch upwards, the concrete cracks covering the vertiginous underworld, can you imagine the young girl's pleasure as she, vested with the power of life over death, ran, helter skelter down the pavement, shouting don't jump on a crack or you'll break your mother's back.

This herpes was going to be painful. A cluster of lumps was forming, like something alive, glowering in her.

The front door bell rang. Amy stood, knees aching, went downstairs.

Hi. Shanara was on the doorstep, dressed in black as always, and a long cream jacket.

Shanara! I tried to ring you. You don't need to come tonight.

Yes, I know, my brother told me. Shanara looked disconcerted. She occasionally looked like that, unsmiling, nervous, anxious to get away. These came for Tom. She handed Amy some letters, I thought I'd bring them.

Shanara, the best babysitter on the street, had returned from a miserable summer in the States, leaving job after job as a nanny when the families unfailingly expected her to take on the rôle of parent substitute. Tom, needing someone to answer the office phone while he and Ruth, his stage director conducted five days of actors' workshops, had offered the job to Shanara.

Every evening that week Tom had bundled back, laughs spilling out of him, about how he and Ruth, and the five actors, had etched away at his script, taking the characters back to the essential, and how every chance they got they fell into jokes about sex, sex of any and every kind, fist fucking, you name it. At one point, two of the actors had danced in, singing, it's nothing but a cliché. And Tom had especially liked their honesty, and had told Amy that unless the script was dangerous, risky, went to the edge, it would not work.

Thanks Shanara. See you tomorrow night, anyway, for Matilda's concert. About six. Come for a drink.

Yes, see you then. Bye.

Shanara was already down the steps, leaving, disappearing into the cold darkness of the solstice, the longest night, December the twenty-second. Seeing *The Sheltering Sky* would have to wait Amy thought as she shut the door. Tomorrow afternoon the rest of Tom's family were arriving. Festivities would be on for the duration.

Amy took the envelopes Shanara had given her into the kitchen. Three were Christmas cards but one, a typed letter, two sheets, folded, had already been opened. Curiously, she looked at it. Tom always showed her his letters, or left them out for her to read if they were from friends. She didn't always pay much attention. They were his letters.

She noticed no address or date. She read, 'Dear Tom,' handwritten and then, typed, 'Tonight I'm alone. Me, myself and I, taking the opportunity to write to you. Transgression, living on the edge, crossing boundaries, obsessions, the other, yes, everything to all that and more that you said. That experience, that existence. For me too, though I'm not sure whether that's how I'll always live.'

Amy felt her cunt expire. Something opened out, gave way. She recognized the impetuous tone, the confident stream of words, the airy chattiness. This was a letter from Lisa. Tall, dark-haired Lisa with the flashing narrow eyes, the upper-class drawl, the sneering shoulders, the graceless attempt, last time Amy had seen her, to sit with Amy and Tom around a table at a restaurant, just before their wedding, or just after. Lisa had been Tom's lover four years ago. She had sent him a Christmas card this year. He had seen her for lunch in the autumn.

It was back in October sometime. Tom talked it over with Amy beforehand and she agreed reluctantly, finding it hard to say why she felt uneasy. It seemed churlish to have qualms. The sexual relationship between Tom and Lisa was in the past, and he was not like Amy, he often told her, he couldn't just let people disappear out of his life. He liked to stay friends. Yes, I suppose so, Amy said, and she looked him in the eye and insisted that he had to have withdrawn in himself from that erotic connection to Lisa. If you tell me it's not like that any more, then yes, see her for lunch. But the night before Tom and Lisa were to meet, Amy did not sleep, and afterwards, when Tom came in from work, she was impatient. Well? she asked, because he said nothing. What? he said, as if he didn't know what she was referring to. How was it? Okay, he said, woodenly. They talked again but she had no more information from him, other than assurances that transforming his relationship with Lisa into a friendship was possible.

Then, around mid December, Lisa's card arrived. Matilda opened it, as she opened all the envelopes at Christmas, one of her seasonal pleasures. It was addressed to Tom.

Perhaps Lisa thought that no one else would open it. But cards were often addressed to Amy or to Tom, at Christmas. Very few were addressed to each of them, and only a few relatives said, Mr and Mrs Tom Drew, or Tom Drew and family. So Matilda opened the envelope containing the card from Lisa, along with the others that came through the letter box that morning, scattered over the plastic cloth on the kitchen table, between the uncleared breakfast plates, the marmalade, the cereal, the mugs. Matilda handed it to her, and she turned it over and read it. It's from Lisa, Amy said, keeping her voice low and sensible. You remember Lisa. Tom saw Lisa a few weeks ago. She borrowed a script of his and wanted to give it back.

Matilda had still been at nursery when Lisa was Tom's lover or rather, when Lisa and Tom were in a relationship, during the year in which Amy and Tom had been separated.

I don't like Lisa, Matilda said suddenly and left the kitchen.

Amy gathered the cards and put them aside so that Tom could read them. She read Lisa's card one more time. Lisa was making a New Year's resolution to write her own play because of Tom's encouragement. She referred to a computer misprint. Maybe that was something Tom had talked about, during that lunch. And at the end 'love from out in the ether'. Out there in desire where Lisa might still be floating, as it were, with Tom? Amy carefully put the card back amongst the others. What she really wanted to do was destroy it.

When Tom came home that evening she told him that a card from Lisa had arrived, that it was intimate and personal and she was confused. It was not like cards from other friends, who always, somehow, included all of them.

While Tom read the cards, she carried the basket of clean clothes upstairs, dumped them on the bed and started to sort and fold them. Tom came into the room, his face beaded with sweat. I've read the card, he said. It doesn't say anything.

What about that bit at the end, about out in the ether?

She's flying off somewhere. She travels. Look I have to have a shower. Ruth handed me a letter today, just as we were leaving, saying how upset she's been because she thinks the play's going wrong. She wants to talk about it. I've been shaken up. First the letter from Ruth, and then this. I've got to have a shower. We can talk later.

Amy, beginning to feel cold, stood in the kitchen reading the typed letter from Lisa, apparently in reply to a letter from Tom. Lisa said Tom's love showed clear and warm, through all he said in his letter and yet didn't say. Lisa must have written the previous night, or the day before, or the night before that, and now, here she was, Amy, reading it, a letter from Lisa in reply to a letter from Tom.

I'm not like you, Tom had said, I can't just drop people, let them disappear out of my life.

What was this, at the bottom of the page? Glee. And 'I suspect Amy knew, consciously or unconsciously and we couldn't help a certain glee.' Amy frowned. It was about an interview that Amy had asked for, with Eleanor. Amy had not known, when she approached her, that Eleanor was a friend of Lisa's. 'Consciously or unconsciously.' Eleanor and Lisa shared a sense of glee about that cancelled interview? Was Tom meant to, as well?

The rest of the letter went by in a blur. There was something about Tom burgling Lisa's space, luxuriating in contradictions, and about Lisa's New Year resolution to make time to start on her own play, thanks to Tom's belief in her.

It was five minutes past six. Tom had to fetch Matilda at six-thirty. Amy went upstairs, opened the door of the spare room and threw the letter at the bed. She said, This came for you. Shanara just brought it, already opened. I'll make some tea.

Tom turned, opened his eyes, gave her a look that was

sleepy then angry, defended, perturbed.

In the kitchen the kettle took an age. Amy doffed a tea bag in a mug, added milk, wondered whether Tom would want sugar, added half a spoon and took it upstairs. Tom, leaning on an elbow, put the tea on the table by the bed.

You wrote to her. You didn't tell me.

Yes, I wrote to her.

Amy walked out of the room, then went back in. Tom said, I have to go and pick up Matilda, as he got out of bed.

I'm extremely angry. I wanted to tear the letter up. I did burn one of her letters, once, back then. One that came for you.

He picked his jeans up off the floor. He held the letter loosely in one hand. We'll have to talk, he said. When I get back.

It says your love shows between the lines. And she's gleeful about the interview I couldn't do, with Eleanor. Why didn't you tell me you'd written?

Amy left Tom and went back into their bedroom. She sat on the floor amidst the presents and paper. She felt extremely thin and shaky and her hands seemed to have gone stiff when she picked up the trick money box, folded paper around it and turned the roll of sticky tape searching for the end. Tom entered. I'm going to get Matilda.

Yes.

We'll talk when I get back.

He left.

Amy continued to search for the end of the tape. There must be a better way of doing this, she thought, but she could not imagine what it would be. Finally she peeled back the end, cut off a piece, stuck it on the parcel, cut another, sealed the parcel, and added it to the bag. She gathered the remaining unwrapped presents and piled them too into the bag. Pain from the herpes flushed her lower back as she stood, dragged the chair to the wardrobe, hid the presents on the top shelf. She went downstairs to the kitchen and took the sprouts out of the fridge.

She has flown and she has fallen.

Amy lies on a firm surface with her knees up, her feet resting on a rug, her shoulders sunk on a pillow. The bottom of her spine is in a thunk of compacted pain.

The osteopath slides an arm under Amy's spine and presses gently upwards. The room is done out in cream paint and a swirly green carpet. The source of the pain, the osteopath explains, is that the fluid leaking out of the spinal disc is putting pressure on the nerve.

Between the paling fence and the flaking blue shed wall, Amy lies face down on the ground, skirt pulled up. The older of the two Evans boys from the flat next door crouches beside her, the younger one by her feet. The older boy is patting her on the buttocks. Pat, pat, pat. Like a gentle slap. Her pants are pulled down. Her bare buttocks are pale, her legs tanned. She looks up, twisting onto her side. Over the top of the paling fence she sees the face of the old man from the ramshackle boarding house, his eyes bleary and glittering, grey white hair sticking up, his mouth open, his lips pink, wet. She pulls up her pants. Quickly, she says to the boys. They run out onto the pavement and down the hill, skirting the block, avoiding their usual route across back gardens and through fences, until they reach the front of the flats.

'Never say bottom,' Amy's mother tells her, 'seat is the word to use. After all, it's what you use for sitting on.'

'I married your mother because she had such a lovely bum,' — slap went her father's friendly hand on her mother's bottom.

Amy put lentils, soaked, into the pan to boil. She peeled sprouts and notched the ends, the way the English do. She put water in the steamer and then the sprouts, and left them next to the stove. She found the right sized carrot and she left it on the cutting board. She lowered the lentils which had been boiling for ten minutes, added Vecon, put them to simmer. She rinsed the brown rice, put the rice in a saucepan and clicked on the gas. She sat down at the table. The plastic cloth shone. She went back to the stove and lowered the rice.

The room seemed very large. Outside, it was dark. She sat down again and stared at the three decorations hanging over the window, a wooden heart the colour of beeswax, a blue hand with a heart-shaped hole in its palm and a buff terracotta star, and then at the branch of conifer from their Christmas tree – decorated and strung with coloured lights – which she had placed in the jug that afternoon. She was waiting. She wondered if Tom had left Lisa's letter upstairs. She moved and sat in the more comfortable canvas chair. She heard the key in the front door, then Matilda's voice calling, Hello, mum, with a slightly subdued note.

She rose and turned on the gas under the sprouts. Matilda, leaving her coat on the bannister, rushed in, put some cake wrapped in a napkin on the table, and rushed out. Have a good time? Yes. She heard the television go on in the front room. Tom came in, took off his jacket and left it on a chair, said it had been a mistake, taking the children to the London Dungeon for a birthday treat. Matilda came back into the kitchen and said, I didn't see the execution, mum. I didn't want to. Grace said I was chicken. I stayed outside, so did Sarah. Grace said blood went everywhere, spattered on the walls. I didn't want to see it.

No, why should you see it.

Matilda left the room again. Tom checked the rice and lentils. He said, They're done. I'll finish this.

She'll want the carrot raw.

He took the meal into Matilda, who sat watching Blind Date. He came back and chose Matilda's usual chair between the table and the radiator, pushing the table out to make room.

Amy pulled the sliding door closed, and sat near it in the canvas chair. She waited. Tom did not speak.

Amy waited. Then she said, Why didn't you say anything about writing to Lisa?

I knew you wouldn't like it.

When did you write to her? After that lunch?

Yes.

Tom stared across the room at the alcove behind the stove.

Amy said, Her letter's the same as before. She doesn't write as if you're with me. She writes as if you were still on your own, and having a relationship that's personal, special, just with her.

We have a friendship.

That letter carries all that feeling that I talked with you about before you had lunch with her.

Tom looked at Amy and away again.

Amy continued. The invisible. It's there. It's an erotic letter. She's relating to you in the same way as before. The letter's flirtatious.

She waited for a moment then she said, Why didn't you tell me you had written?

He repeated that he was trying to put their relationship on a friendship basis, and Amy knew that. He said that's how he felt for Lisa still.

You feel like that about a woman who expresses glee

because I lose some work?

That's a side of her I don't like, said Tom.

The room seemed very big. Its pale apricot walls, curved alcoves, were strangely tomblike and icy.

She's being competitive. She thinks of me as an enemy, because she still wants to be with you.

Tom said nothing.

If someone said something like that about you, I'd be furious. I'd be loyal to you. How can you say you want to explore the possibilities for friendship with someone who's like that about me?

Silence.

She doesn't write as if she's trying to be friends with you or accepting that you're married to me.

She knows I'm with you. Look, it's just a letter.

Amy argued that he was privileging himself in some male or masculine way, claiming the right to such transgression, to a friendship that excluded her, and she was determined in her manner of speaking, not angry, not confused, but confident. He could not claim such a privilege, she said. She refused the rôle he had projected onto her, in the past and possibly now, of being punitive, punishing, of being the one who doesn't allow forbidden pleasures. It was nothing to do with her. She was talking about their relationship as equals. Not something which had masculine, privileged access. She asked, How many times have you written?

A couple of times.

Why did you write to her? Amy heard her voice go quiet. And she's been writing to you?

Yes.

Not here?

To the office.

What's all this about?

You know I can't talk to you about it. You won't let me talk about my sexual feelings.

What do you mean?

I can't talk to you about this without revealing the dark heart of it. What's at the centre of it.

What do you mean?

This is tearing me apart.

Tom stood, walked over to the cupboards lining the other side of the room. He was retreating, Amy saw, as he glanced at her. He turned to stare at the window in which the decorations and the lights shone reflected against the outer darkness.

He said, I'll have to tell you, even if it destroys us.

Amy's father never holds her hand. She walks beside him in bare feet, squeezing out of the way of people leaving the pool, their wet skin glistening, bodies smelling of sun cream and salt, mouths grinning, chattering. Water seeps over the path from the cliffside making a slimy, mossy strip. Jump, her father says. She jumps.

Her father is tight-lipped. She is nervous, excited, expectant. Her tiny feet run to keep up as they make their way along the concrete path between the rocks, the surf and the cliff.

Her light hair curls loosely round her head; her father's is slicked back with Yardley's Lavender Brilliantine. Her father says that waves look sissy on a man. Amy is wearing a plain red swimming costume. Other small girls at the beach wear costumes of patterned cotton bubbled and puckered with elastic like smocking. Fussy, her mother calls them. Amy's costume is made of the same cotton jersey as her father's black trunks, a stretchy cloth which clings and sags when it is wet.

They have left the beach where Amy usually plays in the rippling tailback of waves over the bright sand or in the pellucid shallows of the rock pools. They are going a long way from her mother and the coloured towels and striped umbrellas along a path which snakes round the cliff. Beside her the rocks are bigger and seaweed flaps in the water, and further out where the green swell is building behind the line of breakers, the surfers are flinging themselves onto the crest of a wave about to break, arms flailing as they try to match the water's force with their own, so that when the wave crashes they can surf the way Amy has seen her father surf, stretching his arms forward, shaking his head, checking to see no one's in the way, as he — they — tumble in on a long joyous swing of driving water.

Afterwards her father always comes out snorting, drops of water sparkling on his body. 'That was good,' he says and 'Where are the Capstans?' He likes a smoke after a surf.

She can see the pool. Children run round the wall screaming and jumping in. The high tide has brought the water level up. Adults sit on benches by the cliff. Past the pool the rocks shelve, and the ocean spreads out and up into the sky's indiscernible brilliance, and a ship sails, far, far out, heading south.

Her father puts down the towels on an empty bench. Amy walks silently over to an open path that slopes down into the water. The sides of the pool, white painted over turquoise, are flaking. She makes her way down the slope, keeping near the wall. All around the din of laughter and shouting. The water reaches her swimming costume. Her father says, Wait. He comes into the pool, one leg over the side, then the other, into the water beside her. Come on, girlie, he says, you're going to learn to doggy paddle.

A boy rushes past her. She blinks, surprised, her eyes sting in the water.

Come on, girlie, her father says to her. She stands next to the wall, waist deep. Her father demonstrates.

He holds her tightly, one hand on her tummy, one on her back, pushing her forward into the water. He knows only two ways to hold. Extremely hard and tight, or not at all. Doggy paddle, he says.

When her father swears at the lawn mower, he says, you bitch, and when he calls to their dog, he says, come here, girl, you know I love you.

She digs into the sea water in front of her. He lets go of her. She sinks, chokes, swallows sea water. He takes hold of her again round the waist, his thumbs digging into her spine and leads her back towards the shallow end. Doggy paddle, he says. She arches her neck, trying to keep the salt water out of her mouth, her nose, her eyes. She kicks her legs. He says, Keep your knees straight. Her arms and hands dig and dig. Her movements are useless. She cannot breathe. He does not let go of her. Then he tells her that's enough for one day.

Walking back afterwards was when she saw the crab.

Something that rushed out from between the rocks as they were returning from the pool.

It was like a spider yet it wasn't a spider. It was a hard, encased, shell-like, spiky thing with spiky legs, and a waving pincer, and it was all the colours of the rainbow but mainly blue, gleaming, coloured, wet, shiny and blue. Dad. She could hardly speak.

What?

I saw something.

She looked back at the rocks as they fell away to the water, then aside into the dark cranny of the cliffside, and up where the rocks gave way to grass tufts. It had scuttled across the path so fast her father appeared not to have noticed. It had been like a crab, yet it was not a crab, raised up on its thorny blue black legs, with its claw, and horny eyes.

It had startled her, metamorphosed apparently out of her fear and rage and out of her claustrophobia in the water with her father. Inexplicable terror then attached itself to that hard crablike exterior, nothing vulnerable, exposed, soft.

But how could a child that could hardly speak, talk of this thing? It was as monstrous as a firebreathing dragon in a cave. Was it a daemon? Her own?

Tom turned and gazed directly at Amy. His eyes, she noticed, looked darker, cavernous. I slept with Lisa, three times, last year, he said.

She stared at him. She looked away, desperate. She looked back. There were such a cold quiet in the room. The pale apricot walls pressed back colourless and went absolutely still.

She sat, unmoving, in the chair. She heard herself repeat what he had said. You slept with her three times.

Yes, said the man who stood there, who had been the Tom that she knew and who was now someone else, whose arms hung limp, helplessly, who was looking at her with candour at last — and this seemed to be, to her, then, a key to something, she did not know what, except that it was the start of a true telling of things between them, and so a relief — there was a ground that held and did not sway and shift, mist over, emotionally thick and congealed, like a furred coating or frosting which in the past kept her small and intrusive and always diminished. Tom was leaning back, slightly, against the cupboards. Amy was cold, unshaken. The burning pain of herpes was forgotten. She stood. She said, I'm glad you've told me. She walked towards him. I'm not forgiving you. It has nothing to do with that.

He looked frightened, terrified even, bewildered, lost.

She put her arms around him and held him to her.

He leaned into her.

They embraced.

She had never felt him so close, holding her against him

as he was doing, as if he were frightened she would pull away. She could feel his heart beat through his sweater.

She let go. She thought that although love was possibly mere conceit, something had been reciprocated, some barrier had been broken.

He said, as she went and sat down again in the canvas chair, I thought you'd kill me.

So began a long night.

You three. Amy. Doug. Marie. You three slouchers. Didn't I tell you?

Yes. Out in the front.

See this. What is it?

A broom.

And this.

The handle from the broom.

This broom handle is going to give each of you a straight back. So.

Mrs Lucas, the teacher, hoisted Doug's arms up his back, slotted the broomstick across, between the crook of his elbows.

That's it. That's more like it. Walk in front of the class, Doug. Once. Once only, I said. Now come here.

Mrs Lucas took out the broom handle. Doug's face had gone red.

Amy. Next.

Marie. Next.

Marie went yellower, Amy went greyish.

Amy's hand crept down under her skirt, after, under the desk. She touched herself. Comfort.

Matilda came in and chose a yoghurt from the fridge. To Amy the room still seemed to be emptying, turning from colder to coldest. For Matilda, apparently, it was unchanged – home, comfort, family. Matilda moved calmly, found what she needed, left the room. Tom waited against the cupboards where he had made his announcement, where they had embraced, then he sat down at the table, back in his usual chair. Amy closed the door.

She thought how, as she walked over to hug Tom, her spine held. She was not walking stiffly, nor was she slouching or crouching or flinching. Seated back in the chair, her herpes flared and burned. She shifted, leaned sideways against the flexible, canvas back. The feeling of holding Tom, of his release from whatever had enclosed him in invisibility and withholding all those years, lodged, stayed with her. Otherwise, she thought, she was 'in shock' and 'drained', her reactions on slow, on hold, on stop. She was hollow. Now she knew what the phrase 'hollow men' meant. Who wrote it? Eliot, no doubt, but any knowledge of that sort, literary or otherwise, had vanished.

When? she asked.

February or March, he said, then May, I think, and the last time in August, when you were away with Matilda.

Then, she said, hearing the grim despair in her voice.

Yes, he said, looking at her, acknowledging. I told her then I could not continue with that duplicity at the centre of my life. I had to stop, before it went too far. Lisa always kept herself back. I chose you, and Matilda.

She heard his impossibly formal, abstracted way of saying something difficult. She heard everything he was telling her. That he could perhaps have left her for Lisa and had chosen not to. Instead he had returned to her. She kept herself straight in the chair.

She was quiet. He talked more. He talked of what she knew and remembered.

Before that August holiday, the Tarot card. The Ten of Swords. A prostrate figure, face down, ten swords stuck the length of the spine. Pain. Wounding. She'd looked at it, mystified. She said to Tom she thought something awful might lie ahead, something that would happen when she was away. She did not tell him of the card. The cards did not interest Tom. They were her private game, her private life.

She thought – betrayal – but she could not envisage it.

In the small rented cottage in Wiltshire, Amy slept in one room and Matilda slept in the other. The window was open onto the garden, where cream, pink and apricot hollyhocks flowered in profusion. On the second or third night, Amy turned on the light, unable to sleep. Silhouetted against the blue damask curtain was an extremely large spider. There was something about it being there, like a message, but she could not think what it might be. Unmoving. Defenceless. Terrifying.

Amy left the bed carefully. If Tom were there, he would cup his hand gently over the spider, and put it out the window. She considered. The spider did not deserve to be killed. It was not the threat she felt it to be. What was it? She turned and picked up the morning's newspaper, and folded it. If she were not immediately successful, the spider would scuttle down the curtain, between the bed and the wall, or worse, over the bed, and she would scream, and Matilda would hear, and be terrified.

Amy took aim and hit. She squashed the spider by taking it in one blow upwards, against the curtain rail.

She picked up the pieces with kleenex, trembling. She put them in the wastepaper basket, along with the stained, blotched newspaper.

Later she woke, muzzy with sleep, her eyes burning, unrested and wet with tears. The light shone bluish, already hot, through the curtains. In her dream Tom was with Lisa. She wondered if Matilda was awake. Outside, she thought, green country lanes. No deadlines. No phone.

That was when Tom had last fucked Lisa, when he had decided not to fuck with her again.

Swords piercing the spine. A straying spider. Exigencies. Elements. Dreams.

Wearing t-shirt, pants, socks, Amy waits. She looks at the framed photo on the wall of a white-haired man, dressed in a Victorian coat and waistcoat. He holds a human femur at which he is gazing seriously, gently.

The door opens.

Hello. How are you today? Let me look at you. Stand with your back to me. Bend one knee. Now the other knee.

Amy lies on the table which is at a diagonal across the room. She asks the osteopath about the photo. It was the founder of osteopathy, a doctor whose own children died of meningitis, who discovered that the body responded to massage, whereby the tissues seemed to release self-healing properties. Of course medicine was more primitive then, says the osteopath. It was the glands, the endocrine glands and so on.

The osteopath's hands probe Amy's cervical vertebrae. She moves to the other end of the table, and holds Amy's feet. She stands at the side of the table, pulls up a chair, inserts a hand under Amy's back, lifts the area around the middle thoracic vertebrae. She moves the chair again, slides her hands lower down between the lumbar vertebrae and sacrum. She moves back to the top of the table, presses, holds. Amy flinches, shakes, starts to unwind. Amy laughs as her head involuntarily turns to the side, her right leg turns out and in, then straightens. Like hysteria, in slow motion, she thinks. Good, have a laugh, says the osteopath, it releases the tension. You should change your chair during the day.

Why do you think it happens, this lower back pain?

Anger, says Jill. It's always anger. You know those really polite women, who nevertheless frighten you? They're the type who get it the worst.

Amy, sitting in the canvas chair in the cold, apricot room, said, looking directly at Tom, It's adultery.

I know, he said.

You made it sound as if being married made no difference.

That time when I met Lisa for lunch, that was when I was trying to put the relationship on a different footing. You see. To change it from a sexual relationship to a friendship.

You don't have any guilt.

If you said you wanted to sleep with someone else, I wouldn't stop you.

The other person always wants more, she said. Someone is always going to be hurt.

Until late they stayed in the kitchen. Matilda came back in, talked, went upstairs to bed. Amy did not go up to Matilda's room to say goodnight. She let Tom do it.

Amy asked him when he had first seen Lisa again. He said it was at a first night of a play. He had not told her. Then he had rung Lisa, the next day. They met for lunch. Yes, at her place. Afterwards, they went to bed. Tom had not been able to stay, he said, In my heart I always went back to you.

How can I live through the next few days, said Amy, wondering. What mask would she wear? What had Tom forced her into?

I wrote to her when you wanted to interview Eleanor. I knew she and Eleanor were friends. Somehow I was scared you'd find out.

Eleanor knows?

I don't think so.

How would I have found out?

I don't know. I thought something would happen.

You undercut my livelihood. Even that, Amy said. She sat, quiet. She glanced over at the window. The decorations were turning slightly in the rising heat from the radiator under the window.

You're a liar, she said.

He said nothing. After a while, he asked, Do you want to eat?

No. Then she said, Does anyone know?

Ruth.

You told Ruth?

Yes, I did. She said to me, Your life is in ruins, Tom. Stop it. Stop it right now.

When was that?

Sometime in the summer.

Amy felt bodiless. Images, greyish, black and white, newspaper photos, smudged faces, screen images, moving, came at her. Wives, betrayed. Pitiful, bowed, humiliated. Men as husbands who left, returned, also pitiful, bowed, humiliated. Grey. Dust. Hate. Choking images. She sat, bodiless, straighter, felt the canvas back of the chair tilt. Bodiless. Still, her spine stayed, the finest thread to which she was attached, floating amidst paper images, celluloid. Words came also, from a great distance.

You're weak. You're a liar and a cheat. You've broken vows. You made vows and you've broken them. You've betrayed me. You have no integrity. I can't trust you. I could divorce you.

Yes, he said.

He did not look like the man she knew. She saw someone tall, thin, in jeans and a white shirt, red, curling hair falling forward over his forehead, a man with round blue eyes and a girlish mouth, his top lip full. Shadowed, creased under the eyes. Arms too long even for his height. All the pieces of him she could no longer put together.

She felt tired and said she would eat something.

Tom cooked a tomato omelette and opened a bottle of wine.

She felt no responsibility, no involvement in what he had done.

After eating, in silence, they went to bed. Matilda came in, unable to sleep, then returned to her room. Amy sat, in a t-shirt, on her side of the bed. Tom said, If you feel you're falling into a black hole, tell me.

I'm not, said Amy.

Amy stayed upright, while Tom lay under the duvet beside her.

In the unfamiliar, emptied space she now seemed to occupy, where the connecting threads of home, family, love, care, domesticity, trust, belonging, had been rent asunder, she moved blind, on instinct, waiting for the slightest shift of mood, tone, impetus. The slightest turn of the current. Not knowing what it might be. Only the present, unformulated space around her. She was without carapace or protection. There was only her spine, the thinnest of ridges, all of a piece, flexible, jointed, like green cane in the wind, a whip.

She said, leaning over Tom, I have to do this.

Tom, looking up, saw Amy, in her white t-shirt, saw the fine fluff of her pale hair, like a baby's, which he always found appealing, liking to stroke it sometimes, cradling it. Burning. She frightened him. Her features a skull. White face. Long, pale eyebrows, grey eyes, firing when she spoke.

She gleamed in the pale half dark of the room. She leaned across him fast, pinned his arms, raised her hand and slapped hard.

She contacted his ear, not his cheek. He held her hand away from him with one arm, and with the other protected his face. She wrenched her hand out of his clasp and hit again, aiming at the other cheek.

Don't he said.

Let me, she said. I have to.

Afterwards she lay back. The palm of her hand stinging, hurting dully.

I have to know, she said, the actual dates.

Tom could not remember.

What had he done with the letters?

He had destroyed them.

What had he felt, afterwards?

The first time, he said, he was frightened. He blanked it out.

To know, to understand, to have the facts, thought Amy. Like a lawyer. Sift evidence. Seek. Understand.

She had to make him retrieve.

Disgust, horror, distaste, as she asked questions while the spine, the ridge, held, a thread of beaded bone.

By dawn she understood. His words hid the truth. Words, for him, were the fuel, the energy. A playwright he was and always would be. He had said I chose to stay with you, and he meant he might have chosen to stay with Lisa. His fantasies had lain long with Lisa, and when, at last, he had fucked Lisa again, his fantasies had fluttered, died. But Amy realised that between him and Lisa it was no longer the same. He would not have stayed with Lisa. It was not that he stopped it while he and Lisa were still able to stop it. He and Lisa would not have ended up together. It was not an equal contest, between Amy and Lisa.

His words were not the event. The act was not the one he had spoken of, or implied.

You don't love her, said Amy although, she thought, she no longer knew what the word love meant.

She could not think in what manner it might have meaning again. She lay down, at dawn, under the dark green duvet, on the pine bed. She shuddered. She was cold, tired. She slept. Tom slept.

It was Christmas Eve. Ivy decorated the church, and there were candles, and the deacon, a woman, sometimes called God 'She'. Amy sat beside Tom. The vicar strode along the aisle. 'Faith,' he bellowed. 'Frank Sinatra said he'd believe anything that'd get him through the night.' Faith, thought Amy, always elusive. It no longer mattered, somehow. They had each wanted to attend the service. The herpes blisters were visible now, and the pain less. Sitting on the hard bench, she was pleased to be there.

She carried Matilda's stocking into the bedroom, nibbled the biscuit put out for Father Christmas, and left. She went to their bedroom, got into bed. Tom came in, lifted the duvet, lay next to her. He reached over. Amy lay still, quiet. The candles they had brought away from the church, relit, flickered in the room. Tom held her. He touched her, and touched lycra. She had not completely undressed. She lay passive and unresisting, as though she were dead, had just been killed. Tom was surprised. Delicately, confidently, he kissed her. He made his way through her underwear. She came to life wherever he touched, wherever he felt, explored, caressed.

He had pierced, in desperation, by betrayal, the crablike

exterior which had guarded and concealed her from him.

The thermometer on the verandah reads 38°C. What's that in Fahrenheit? Amy asks. I don't know, her mother says, going inside.

She sits with one leg folded over the other, sweating. Between her legs her skin is slippery. A black, white and red butterfly flutters back and forth between the verandah pillars and the shining, swaying needles of the Mexican pine. The breeze is a rearrangement of heat. It cools, though, drying the sweat under her armpits, as she sits, thinking.

She's had a letter from Tom. She has left, temporarily, to consider what to do. He wrote that he dreamed of a young girl who looked rather like Matilda or a younger Amy. In the dream he had a fine metal thread which he pulled, tightly, around the young girl's neck. He watched her as he pulled. Tightly and more tightly until he throttled her. She was dead. He had strangled her.

Then she looked back at him. She smiled. She was alive again, and she was smiling at him, in his dream.

And that same morning, Matilda had told him of a dream she had the night before. Matilda dreamed there was a large spider, on her hand, she could just see its legs. She screamed and screamed for Tom to come and take it away. He did. She woke, relieved.

Tom rang Amy in Australia. He rang at nine in the evening, English time. She was eating breakfast. 'When are you coming home?' he asked.

'Am I coming home?'

'Aren't you?'

FOR ESTELA

BE MY BABY

Marina Warner

The blanket was one of the standard issue white cellular sort they wrap babies in, and I could see through the holes though nobody could see my face as I was coming out. The pinpricks like stars with people in bits behind them made me think how it was when I used to go to confession and Father Sylvester was just a shape behind the screen like a ghost, though in this case I was the ghost, that's what I looked like in the photos the press took all the same, even though you couldn't see anything of me except a white blob, a Halloween prank, with the police around towering over me, they were old-fashioned in their height, I wondered about that. I like a tall man, I like to feel little. Andrew used to call me his little chickadee, his baby bunting and sweet petnames like that and though he isn't exactly a big man, he had a nice pair of broad shoulders on him, and I could make him feel really big, you know, inside me, he liked that about me, that I could get him so excited he'd shout he could shaft a horse. I could see the mouths of the pressmen opening and shutting, they were calling out to me, wanting to have a good peek, but I wasn't going to let them, what was in it for me? Besides I don't give myself away to just anybody, like

Sister Richard used to say, save up your treasure on this earth, and you'll lay up more treasure in heaven. And we all know what she was talking about. One-track minds, the nuns, in spite of their sheltered life.

Near the courtroom, one of the police, it was the woman detective, she held on to my arm, really tightly, she was hurting me. And I was already handcuffed to her. She was walking me fast into the building from the van saying I'd have to tell my story later, most likely, but not yet. I could see more mouths opening and shutting through the gaps in the blanket, it was like a net and they were fishes gasping and I'd caught them. But I didn't hear what they said, though the words thumped me inside like when I bring someone round from a heart attack, making my pulse race and a leaky feeling deep down, like fear but not as nice as the big dipper when it plunges and your innards go all melting. Because it isn't true what they were saying. I love my baby girl, and I know how to look after her really well and I did look after her, there wasn't a spot on her, she was brighteyed and bushytailed when they found us and took . . . and that's a right sight more than you can say about half the mothers I see around me on a daily basis.

'Rowena isn't the right woman for me,' that's what Andrew said over and over, I know he did. I should have been having the baby instead of her, it was his unspoken thought, I know it was, I could always read his mind, he was easy and I could feel how unhappy he was. Of course, then everything could work out for the two of us, I saw it, instantly. I like Rowena, she's good fun, especially when she's a bit oiled, and she's that often enough. I sympathise with her, she's got a problem, who hasn't? She's the frigid sort. We call it vaginismus, I told Andrew, we get patients in all the time with it clenched tight like whelks. You can warm a speculum as long as you like, and coax them, Relax relax, massage their tummies and even stroke the inside of their legs, but you can't get it into them, no way. Anyway Andrew says that when he does get it in, he feels like Napoleon marching to Moscow and it's about as cold and bleak and . . . I shouldn't say it . . . huge in there as the steppes of Russia in winter. These poor women who are past it, one minute they're so tight you'd need a screwdriver to prise them open, the next they're gaping, no control. The vagina walls all slack. I mean Andrew says that as soon as she was pregnant, she wouldn't let him touch her breasts any more, not that she's got much to offer in that department, and she wasn't exactly overgenerous before in what she allowed him. It hurts, she'd say. Well, that's not much of a turn-on, is it? I couldn't tell her, Sweetheart, he fits me to a T. I gave her a tube of gel and told her to hire a video. It was really peculiar to be counselling her how to get off on her own husband specially seeing as he's a real tomcat when it comes to me.

Conjugal duties, we were taught about that. I remember Sister Richard putting a question to us: If your husband was suddenly posted abroad, to India for instance (I can't think how she'd think anyone'd be going there, more like the other way about, they all come here, England's still a great place, even though I switched to private when I started working for Andrew in the clinic, nothing can beat the National Health) – so, if your old man's off to India, do you go with him or do you stay behind and look after the children? Well, I think most of us girls answered, Stay behind for the kids. Being mothers was the big thing, after all, they were always drumming that into us at the convent, the good Lord gave us the equipment so we could have babies. Not just for fun, young ladies. No way. That's right, I still think that. But it turned out that we were wrong,

Sister Richard pointed out that our duties lay first and foremost with our husband, we had to follow him to the four corners, never mind the kiddies, leave them in a home, or preferably with granny, because otherwise your man's immortal soul will be at risk, occasions of sin everywhere, all those invitations to the flesh issued by natives, the females of the species in their gaudy getups with their funny smell like curry – actually Andrew loves curry, the hotter the better – you had to save him from that. Otherwise you'd become a kind of occasion of sin yourself, by omission, like not waking up to a patient's bell the first time and finding when you do get there that you're too late and she's lying in a pool of urine or worse and so ashamed she tells she wishes she'd croak and couldn't you help her? I think the geriatrics had the same effect on Andrew as on me. He said something about the front line of decay and death, about nature asserting herself to preserve humanity. Anyhow Andrew sometimes has to push me up against the wall, or over a table or once up against the drug cupboard just as I was getting out some temazepane for one of the old dears who'd had a bad night. I never had time to put the bottle down but had it in my hand throughout, he was that urgent.

I had to lift the blanket when I got into the court, but the magistrates had cleared the room, so there was just me and them and the police – and, yes, the lady solicitor, and it was funny, because first they charged me with something and then she objected to that because that section of the law had been repealed she said. A right muddle. Anyway then they got the right law and the right section and the right offence according to their way of thinking and hers and they all looked pleased as Punch saying that I did take without lawful authority or reasonable excuse a child under one year from the lawful control of her mother and her father. I saw red, when I heard that, I know the kind of people Opal's so-called mother and father are, the idea that those freaks are lawful and I'm not is just a farce, but my lawyer said I really couldn't talk, that I'd have a chance later, at the proper hearing, this was just committal proceedings. I'm still waiting. Meantime I'm stuck in the bin with a whole lot of perverts and sex maniacs and I'm certainly not going to give any of them the time of day however much the doctor says, Let's include Norma, or asks me if I have any thoughts on the subject in hand. I've got plenty of thoughts, I can tell you, but I know that doctors most of the time know much less than the nursing staff and would get nowhere without Sister especially to tell them what to do, so I'm not going to fall for his tricks, and certainly not in that company. One of the men is a — I can't spit it out — no better than an animal and one of the women who was giving us her life story yesterday with lots of bawling — crocodile tears if you ask me and a bid for attention — she's a pro. and she's been one since she was twelve years old and her mother put her on the game. Well, I felt a little stab of sympathy when I heard that. Typical, I thought. But I wasn't going to let her past my guard, because if you have a mother like that you're lost from the start. I could feel sorry for her, but she's still rotten right through to the core, might as well have terminal cancer for what her chances are, and the rot would've set in irreversibly when she'd have been about three. I used to worry about Susan and Mandy coming back from school on their own, I used to warn them about men making approaches, I'd feel an idiot talking about sweets from strangers, but the things you read in the newspapers about vice rings made me scared for them. Mandy was such a pretty little girl with her fair hair I used to do for her in a

French braid. Maybe that's why she's working in a salon now I haven't seen her since she was . . . well, she's grown up now, she's left the home where they placed her. It was the best, the bedrooms were newly painted she said when she phoned me one time. That's when I had to go private and start night shifts, after I'd given Terry his marching orders because I'd had it up to here with him and anyways that was what I had to do, everyone said so, it was better for the kids too in the long term, than to be growing up with a brutal father who'd bash you soon as look as you when he's fed up with the night's viewing on the telly. There comes a time when you've had enough –

It's down to the mothers, just the same. That's our burden, and our glory. Andrew says that Rowena's feeble, and that's no good, if you can't say boo to a goose you certainly can't cope with a kid. Mothers are a lousy lot and getting lousier, I think you'll agree, I said so to my lady solicitor, and she asked me to go on, she was taking notes, I could see she was listening and nodding, she probably comes into contact with dreadful people most of the time, seeing as the law deals with criminals and perverts . . . not always, of course and in the medical profession there's a few normal people around and the old dears, of course, they're not in the clinic for anything we don't talk about. Though I've had some crazy times, sometimes, that's another story. Mothering's a skill that's in decline, I told her, like home cooking and turning collars and darning socks along with the graceful old dances like the quickstep and the waltz which we were taught at the convent so that we'd have all the accomplishments young ladies need to keep a man happy. She took it all down on her yellow pad. Dreadful handwriting, lucky I'm a nurse and can read anybody's scrawl so I could see she was making extra notes about what I was telling her. Not bad but mad? Not bad but mad? she had the nerve to scribble and think I wouldn't understand. I just laughed at her. I'm biding my time.

At first I wasn't sure about the underwear, it made me giggle, the knickers with the bit between the legs cut out, the 'love gusset' the label called it, the bras with holes for your nipples to poke through. He left this Valentine Mailorder book for me with a really sweet note, he said, 'For my baby bunting, with a big wet kiss from Daddy Bear.' No name of course, just in case, you never know who's snooping around, and at first I didn't want anyone to know about us, because, well, he didn't want to hurt Rowena, he's a decent man, and she was having Robert and she was getting on and he didn't want the baby upset either. Impressions in the womb count, he's right to be careful, it begins before birth even, the influence of the parents.

He was always saying, 'There's the baby to consider.'

In the last place where I worked I had my tubes tied, I'd never told Andrew that, didn't get a chance to, we had better things to talk about than my medical history, I can tell you, but after the three kids I felt enough is enough, it seemed right at the time, and Terry was ever so keen, there was the one I'd lost too. The girls were growing up so we'd have to split them from Sammy and put him somewhere else, in the living room, or in with us again. The council kept on saying we'd be rehoused, and when I started working nights it was hard to get them off to school on time they were in such a mess without me around to clean up. I know the Pope says it's wrong to have your tubes tied, and I see why now, but the girls we have in at the clinic for the DNCs could do a lot better if they went the whole hog and got sterilised, then they wouldn't be killing their babies after they're formed, all perfect in miniature I've seen them on the spatula. And I mean when you see the little thing wriggle on the sonar scan and you can even spot its willie if it's a boy it's a right sight different from shedding the ovum before it's fertilised I think, I don't like working on terminations but I have to hand it to them, these patients at least admit they're no good at being mothers, which is more than most of the ones walking around with dozens of kids already and another one in the pipeline.

I asked about getting them untied. It's not like a vasectomy, though. Men have all the luck, lucky devils I say they are, even in something like this, snip snip, they're back to normal, but in my case, no go, what's done's done.

At Christmas Andrew had the office party in his house. I encouraged him, it'd be a real treat for all of us, and I told Rowena we'd all be on good behaviour, I'd see to that, I'd keep the little SENs in line, no spilt drinks on her new shagpile, no rings on the French polish. It was really fancy, outside catering, tree on the lawn, nothing routine like multi-coloured fairy lights, no, all in silver, with snowflakes like stars lit up. When Rowena tucked up early, she was tired, she was near full term and almost everyone had left and those that hadn't were past caring, we had a secret session in the sauna room, it was really erotic slithering on the wooden slats, slapping around with the towels with the steam hissing and then the cold water, whoosh, like a rush of amyl, it was straight out of a video. Andrew that night wasn't like a man of fifty something, I told him, he was a young billy goat, honest. Then he was lying quiet. I love him more like that, when he's almost like a baby, and I stroked him and dried him and helped him back into his clothes again and combed his hair, and he was all tender and docile, like a patient who gives no trouble to the staff and I knew I had to make the decisions for us. Men are like children, it's a cliché but that doesn't stop it from being true. They can't take a step without someone holding them by the hand, That's right, put it down there, now there, well done, until they can crow, Look, I'm doing it, all by myself. So I thought, Andrew can give us a good home, more than Terry ever could, I shouldn't have even tried to make a family with him, but I was young then and I was clueless, I admit it. But now, now that I've got the full benefit of experience, I can live my life again, I mean men are always doing it, getting married and messing up and then starting again. The kids are grown up now, Susan's got a bloke already, Mandy's in the salon, Sam'll be out of school soon into VTS, they have programmes now for school leavers better than in my day, and I'm only thirty-two. I've got my whole life still ahead of me, I said to myself. I'm free to choose a new one. That's what I'm telling myself, lying there on the boards in the sauna with Andrew like a lovely big baby who's had a really good feed lolling against me all blissful like with a little smile twitching in the corner of his mouth, which may have been the beginning of a snore, just like an infant who's not really smiling, just having a bit of wind and the silly mother goes all cooey and gooey because she thinks a baby of ten weeks already knows how she's mum and is smiling at her for special.

Some of these mums beat belief: I stop now and give them a really good stare so that they can see that someone is paying attention to their carry-on. You'd think children were as hard to handle as a Tornado fighter plane the fuss they kick up in public to win sympathy and attract attention, the way they crash and go up in flames at the least opportunity, yanking at their kids and shouting blue murder. Well, they don't get my sympathy, but I notice. I'm building up a file on your little lot, I feel like saying. Only I don't, I keep quiet, biding my time.

You can break the new mums down into several sorts, there are the whingers, the ones who go snivelling along behind their pushchairs, saying I'm at the end of my tether I haven't got the money for another Ninja turtle I might have tomorrow if you're good. Then there are the glamourpussies, the ones who hang about together smoking with their long red nails glinting checking their gloss lipstick contours in their compacts while in the pram — this lot always have the fanciest cabriolet style navy blue and gold jobs with four gear suspension — their elder offspring is choking the baby sitting on his face or beating him up and meanwhile mum's puffing away passing the time of day with her friend, Dick this and Ron that and Franny this and Myra that. Do you really think women like that deserve to have kids? And I won't even get on to so called one-parent families who invite child abusers right into the bedroom and say, Yes, sweetheart, go right ahead, bugger my baby, stick your finger right in there, doesn't that feel nice. God, I sometimes wonder if you still exist or whether the redemption has run out, like money in a meter, it's nearly two thousand years since God so loved mankind he gave his only begotten son to die for us and maybe the effect is fading. Sometimes I felt that I didn't have the strength to keep on loving enough to hold me and Andrew and Opal together, when he didn't come and visit us that time the way he said he would and didn't call until the next evening and then muttered about things had come up at the clinic and he'd got held back in the office, I was a bit upset, I had to summon up all my energies to push down the bitterness I felt swelling up inside. But I was just sweet to him down the phone, I didn't want Opal to hear any disagreement between her father and mother as she was peacefully lying in her cot in that halfway state babies lie in, with their eyes open, looking but not looking, must be the way our consciousness is when we're bodiless, like the saints in heaven. Of course, Opal isn't bodiless, and I take care of all that side really well, even the people in the town when I went out commented what a beautiful baby she is. I called her Opal because it's my birthstone, I was born on November the twenty-second, feast of Saint Cecilia, that's why I like music, Sister Richard used to say. Opal and me have the radio on often, we go dancing together, that's how I describe it to her, bobbing up and down with her against me to Marvin Gaye.

I put together a really beautiful layette for her, nothing but the best, took the coach to London one Saturday I had off, before Opal, but when I already knew, knew as certain as day is day and night is night that the time was coming when I'd have her all my own, and I went into The White House, Bond Street, W.1, which is *the* place for baby clothes since Queen Victoria, I was calm as you please and asked for a recommended list of layette items, the shop assistant was very accommodating. Madam, she said, and showed me the newborn section, because she could see from my shape I was soon due. There's this linen romper suit with écru smocking, Madam, and mother-of-pearl buttons, so I pointed out to her that these'd dig into a baby's flesh when she's asleep. She was showing me more from a drawer behind the counter and displaying them for me in a pile on the glass top. There were so many, she said nuns in Portugal embroidered them, they still had the nimbleness in their fingers to do tiny details and the patience as well. It wouldn't have been good for someone who didn't know to have the romper suit the way it was, and when I got home I cut off the buttons and put nice flat poppers instead and it was such a lovely hot summer that when I put Opal in the stroller with the lace parasol I picked up in Mothercare and she was wearing her romper suit with the écru smocking so that her sweet soft knees with the dimples in them peeped out, we stopped the traffic, I'm telling you, and that's not easy in this country where most everyone behaves like children were a bad smell under their noses.

Andrew was a bit surprised when I told him about the baby, but he gave me some money — he's a real gentleman when it comes to the open chequebook — and he was pleased I found a cottage in the village so quickly. I've got good stomach muscles I told him, when he was investigating, they just snap back like suspenders I said. Rowena was still baggy, I could see him thinking, I can always read his thoughts, seven months since her baby boy Robert was born and she hadn't recovered her shape such as it was. I bought flowers for the little table in the window nook and made chicken vindaloo with real crisp poppadums the way he likes and Opal was good as gold in her Moses basket. He said she had a very nice-shaped head, which is true, I wouldn't have a forceps delivery, even a low forceps, I know what that can mean in the long run. No, Opal was born full of the joys of spring, easy birth, four hours after the waters broke, no epidural even, I made sure by reading the notes on her because I couldn't remember anything myself, not afterwards. The notes were in the babies' changing room, one of the nurses left to answer a call and she had them with her. I remember talking to yet another of those taffyhead girls — another single parent, of course — who'd just let the world roll over her and brought a child into the world without knowing one end of a baby from another. All she could talk about was her stitches itching and the size of her boobs and the milk flooding. Opal was lying on the changing mat waving her arms and legs and I knew she'd be better off without such a person rabbiting on about herself instead of dedicating herself to the job before her. She hadn't an idea what it meant of course and I didn't see it as my task to straighten her out on the subject. I was going to care for Opal and give her my full attention.

There was a nice cot with Furry Forest Folk painted on the headboard in the Mothercare book and I hadn't managed to get a cot, you can't wheel one out of the shop like you can a buggy and bring it home on the bus so I showed the picture to Andrew and he said, Go ahead, and he wrote me another cheque for a bit over the cost of the cot, and I almost came over funny, because he was committing himself to us, when she got to be the right size she was going to sleep in a bed chosen by me and paid for by her father and it was only a matter of time, I just had to be patient and loving and I'd be requited in full measure. Like the nuns used to say, still waters run deep and the mighty shall be cast down and the meek shall inherit the earth. It would all come to Opal and me in the end because we deserve it.

I caught the news on the telly with a Photofit that didn't look in the least bit like me and I saw the girl and her boyfriend pretending to cry so that they could screw some money out of the papers and the fool public who come over all soft when they see tears in a so-called mum's eyes. I hugged Opal really tight and put the radio on and got a Golden Oldies station and I danced with her holding her close and it was one of the sweetest times of my life – someone, was it The Ronettes? – they were singing all these sweet nothings and I repeated them softly, singing along with the, oh yes, she's my baby, my very own, and I was never going to let her go. I really never expected to be so happy not ever ever it was like a big light shining inside me and setting me all aglow to have Opal mine to care for and bring up right. I went to mass with her in the snuggly – I hadn't been for a long time but I wanted to talk to Our Lady and the saints and baby Jesus and I got down on my knees I'm telling you to say thank you to them for Opal's life and mine and Andrew's and to pray to them to give us all a chance to thrive together. Thrive is the word, failure to thrive that's what people say about children with the wrong kind of mothers, Terry repeated it to me one time I remember.

The doctor at the therapy group asks me if I've got any more feelings about Our Lady and her being on my side. She was a single parent, too, he says. Which just shows how much he knows his gospels since her marriage to Joseph is written down there plain as day. I told him in no uncertain words. Then one of the perverts said that I was an unmarried mum myself with Opal if you accepted that she was mine in the first place which she wasn't and I tried to break in and stop his dirty mouth but the doctor let him speak and he went on, he's an inarticulate brute stumbling over his words as if his teeth didn't fit under his lips and he said that Andrew couldn't have married me for ages seeing as he was married already and the quickest divorces take a year so that technically I was a single-parent family too. I shot him down in flames. That's what it might be 'technically' I said but what does love have to do with 'technically'? He said, You're really confused, and the doctor then shut him up which was about time. But I was upset, they were driving a wedge between me and Opal and between me and Andrew and that's when I asked the doctor if I could have the blanket back so that I didn't have to see them all except in little bits and pieces which makes them manageable the way you just uncover a portion of the patient's body during an op so the surgeon can work without being disturbed by stupid distractions happening elsewhere.

He protested but not very strongly and asked the nurse to bring me one, and I feel much better now wrapped up with everything that's not inside my head muffled and screened off. There was a paper in the corridor with that stupid idiot girl on the front – she should be making toothpaste ads – and the headline was like the doctor but saying more loudly that Opal was her baby and I had to go along with it.

But I know she's still safe and warm inside with me, she sucks the corner of her white blanket when she's hungry and I'm preparing her feed. I always use the thermometer to get the temperature just so and change the steriliser water more often than the instructions say, even though they're only keen to make money out of babies and don't really have their health at heart.

I know the smell of her apricot soft skin and her little wet mouth like a rosy sea anemone – Sister Richard used to say the nun's was the highest calling, but that motherhood wasn't far behind.

THE ECLIPSE OF THE FULL MOON

Alison Fell

1963, THEA

Four girls, Lilli, maybe ten years old, in white dresses, seated around a table which is covered by a white tablecloth: you and I, and two others whose names the dream forgets. The table stands on a terrace which stretches away to a horizon ridge of snow-corniced mountains. The girls eat from white china plates, unsupervised and tidily. A silver-blue fish lies on a plate, a knife slices it transversely, and suddenly there is colour: the pink burst of bougainvillaea as the skin parts and blossoms spill from the belly, the orange of azalea, the flame red of the African tulip-tree. The fish on its plate isn't a centrepiece, Lilli; it occupies one place only and that place is yours. While we other girls sit symmetrical as Doric columns in our smocked white dresses and white stockings and hidden white petticoats, watching, yes, just watching, tell me what you make of that, Lilli.

When I was a girl my mother admonished, Don't go to the Bioscope, Thea, you'll ruin your eyes. The Bioscope had a vast dome like a bare breast and that's where I spoiled myself, Fridays, Saturdays, lost Mondays when my mother thought I was in school. The eyes of Bara were kohl-black elongations which ended in arrowheads and her mouth was taut and tender as a wound. How I marvelled at the ranked spears of the Roman Legions, Lilli, and the strong bare legs of the soldiers. How I yearned for a sawn skirt of leather, for a breastplate embossed with a great bronze eagle. Dreaming, I was pierced by an Egyptian spear and bled; in the morning blood covered the sheets and my mother stood in the doorway lightly slapping the cellar keys against her thigh. Tush, Thea, tush.

Nightly my mother stands guard over my orifices, Lilli, watching their issue and judging it; nightly she is a pot into which I empty myself, squeezing, and as turds fall into the water only a small sigh of protest admonishes me, soft as a breath of pollen from a pine cone. Tush, Thea, tush.

Blind I may be, Lilli, but the images in my dreams are as vivid as ever. No, more so. My eyes are the eyes of Bara, peering into an Egyptian tomb. I falter on the lip, a filmy veil drawn across the lower half of my face. Down in the pit there are three cool black stones, and when a voice from below warns me that a body is about to be brought up, I cower back, hiding my face with my hands.

And whose body is it to be, Lilli? That's what I don't know, for that's when my sleep is interrupted by the sound of coffee cups — Ilse is a good girl but in the mornings she does clank so, and her voice when she enters with the breakfast tray is garishly cheerful, drowning out birdsong — that's the question that is never answered, Lilli. Oh, no doubt you will say, after Rilke, that one must not be forever demanding answers, and must learn instead to love the very questions themselves . . . but that's asking too much of me, Lilli, just as you habitually asked too much of yourself. If only humanity could accept its imperfections, you used to say, and live in brotherliness. I can't see, therefore, what led you to set yourself above the rest of us, what led you to that martyr's choice (such enormous self-regard there, Lilli, such an underhand egotism), I simply can't see it.

1975, ILSE

Every morning after the coffee things have been cleared I open the window to let the fresh air blow in from the lake, and I sit at her bedside and read to her. I have to make my voice professional, but that's easily done, and it's really quite interesting — some of the mummies had bunions, you know, just like us nurses. As for making mistakes — which you do, of course, when your eyes get tired and maybe you read 'historical' instead of 'histological' — well, Frau Holstein's come to be such an expert that she's on to me in a flash. And I daren't skip a word or two either, or miss out a sentence, for the blind do have a sixth sense and she notices right away. Listen, Otto, this is how it goes. Dry, isn't it?

> Nowadays the search for disease in the archaeological remains is facilitated by the use of an endoscope, which makes internal examinations possible without massive openings being made in the body. A great deal has been learnt about disease in ancient man in this way. For example, a Peruvian body of the Tiahuanoco period showed worms still clearly attached to the inner surface of the gut. Under the scanning microscope the morphology showed distinctly that this was none other than the destructive hookworm, which causes bleeding and serious anaemia. The body of a priest from Amun (1085–945 BC) showed a serious tubercular infection of the spine with collapse of some of the bones, while histological

> studies on the rehydrated soft tissue of the mummy of Nekht Ankh (1841–1786 BC) showed that he had suffered from pleurisy and pericarditis . . .

The photographs are gruesome, of course, but Frau Holstein won't be spared a single detail. Imagine having to describe the body of a little Eskimo boy, eyeless, his face stretched like parchment, his dark fringe still sticking out of the fur hood of his parka. His poor little hands were dried to claws, Otto, and his little legs and feet were wrapped up in hide leggings and bootees. Honestly, he was so pitiful I almost wept to see him, and my voice trembled thinking of the mother who'd had to bury her darling boy. But Frau Holstein didn't move a muscle, Otto, I don't know how she does it. She has that perfect skin, still: very smooth and soft, like a snowdrift, so that you think if you pressed it with your finger the skin would keep the dent, you know, like the blank eye of a snowman. Oh, but have you ever heard anything as morbid as this bit about embalming, Otto? Just listen.

> Since Egyptian embalmers had a penetrating understanding of decomposition processes, evisceration became common, as did the extraction of the brain through the nose. Aware that shrinkage and drying would occur, the embalmers tried to retain the original body-shape not only by packing the body cavity with straw but also by modelling and by inserting false breasts, penises, etc. into the wrappings. By the New Kingdom (1470–1070 BC) more advanced procedures were being developed in which internal organs were washed, soaked in natron and hot resin, and packed into jars. Toe- and finger-nails were tied on to make sure that they did not fall off during any stage of the process and elaborate packing, application of resin to the

> skin, and bandaging followed. In Oceania, body cavities were stuffed with palm pith and the body hung on a wooden framework to dry, when artificial eyes were fixed in position and red ochre applied to the skin . . .

And then Frau Holstein always has to know exactly what the eyes are made of: are they wood, carved and painted, or coconut or cowrie shell, or emerald or amber? If I tell her that the book doesn't specify, she says, Well find out for me, *Liebchen*, find out. Write it down, she says, for she doesn't trust me to remember. Write it down, Ilse. Addresses of embalmers, that's the latest. I told you there's to be a new will tomorrow, didn't I? The notary is coming all the way from Munich. Frau Holstein has to be dressed by nine and I'm to serve lunch on the terrace if it's fine so that Herr Molders can admire her precious view across the Bodensee to Switzerland.

—

1991, MINNA

Here in Munich the libraries are full of her. *Mountain-Climbing as Metaphor in the Films of Thea Holstein. History as Theatre – the Documentaries of Thea Holstein. Holstein as Auteur.* And so on. Biographies, critiques. Monographs, apologias, rehabilitations. As for you, Lilli, not a trace in the files or on the shelves. No entry in any catalogue for Lilli Kirchner, psychoanalyst, born 1903, died Sachsenhausen 1944. Not a single word to be found. If it weren't for these nightly talks with Uncle Franz – Franz who loved you, Franz who survived – I might begin to doubt that you ever existed. Daily I walk the streets of the city, holding my Stadtplan flat across my chest like a shield against the east wind, following Franz's directions. To the squat block of the

Hospital on Langestrasse, where you trained under the eagle eye of Doctor Kessel; to Honigstrasse, where your old apartment building is being demolished to make way for a Sports Centre; to the Marienplatz at the heart of the city, where townspeople congregate on café terraces to tell their tales. Seeing as I walk not this modern Munich grown fat and sleek on Euro-commerce, but the Munich of the 30s, a Munich half-dreamt, constructed of longing, a convergence of streets teasingly familiar: trams, wagons drawn by horses, corners round which at any moment might come handcarts piled high with mattresses and mirrors and fantastic chests of drawers. Your Munich, Lilli.

1931, LILLI

Out on the Marienplatz that night the air had been sharp with the first chill of autumn, but inside the Town Hall the packed upper gallery was hot and stuffy and smelled heavily of perfume. On the hard oak pew next to Lilli her employer's wife, Frau Kessel, flapped a glove at a fur-coated matron several rows in front and contorted her face into an expression which from a distance might have made the sure sign of a smile but which, close up, was comical in its exaggeration. 'Husband's the *Bankhaus* Meusel,' she whispered in excited shorthand. 'Introduce you later.' It was Frau Kessel's habit to attend each and every gathering at which the well-meaning well-to-do might be found, on the basis that those who contributed to one good cause could reasonably be expected to contribute to another — that is, to the cause of the Herr Doktor and his Hospital, which in Frau Kessel's ardent heart were one and the same. Sometimes Lilli wondered if the aloof Herr Doktor appreciated his wife's efforts on his behalf: the way she scurried in and out of the houses of the very rich, to tea-parties and *Musikabende* alike, soliciting donations. Fortunately for her own peace of mind Frau Kessel was thick-skinned enough not to notice the shrug which accompanied the bank cheque or promissory note, or the cool glance which speculated on ancestry. Lilli, unfortunately, was not, and it was painfully clear to her that those Horvaths and Von Papens tolerated her employer's wife with barely concealed contempt.

Fanning herself with her programme, Lilli tried once again to concentrate on the speeches, on Frau Polster and her soup kitchens and the Fresh Air Fund which whisked poor city children off to farming families for the grace of good butter and salt bread and daily exercise in the sweet-smelling Bavarian meadows. It had been a shock to see Thea's name, so stark and black at the top of the posters, and to wonder what sort of naïvety or calculation had led her to lend Frau Polster's group her backing — for without it, Lilli was sure, the tinpot *Frauenführerin* from Munster would never have attracted such a crowd. Lilli gazed round the hall, exasperated. She could not make sense of it. Surely Thea would feel as bored and fretful as she did at the sight of these ranks of right-thinking burghers' wives?

Down on the platform Frau Polster stood with one hand on her hip, while with the other she pointed, pleaded, cradled imaginary infants. It was the hand on the hip, however, that caught Lilli's attention: the knuckles which dug into the waist, the fingers which swooped back like the frozen wings of the cupids on the proscenium arch. Lilli's thoughts drifted to her patients: Herr Unterheimer with his little feet which stuck up, rigid, at the bottom of the couch; Frau Kruckman, whose jaw was set hard and who recited her afflictions in a bitter monotone. It was difficult to feel any affection for

Frau Kruckman, more difficult still to see how she might be cured. (Not difficult at all, on the other hand, to love the children in the Psychiatric Ward, the children whose underground tremors were so apparent: Skinny suicidal Hans with his big wild hands warding you off; Lucy of the cleft palate and beautiful sea-blue eyes, little Lucy the nurses shook their heads over. Later, looking back, you told Franz that only those Mondays and Thursdays at the Hospital made up for the gloomy hours in the consulting room on Maximilianstrasse and the sclerosis of the patients the Herr Doktor consigned to you.)

Down on the stage Frau Polster regarded the audience for a forbidding moment. 'Friends,' she intoned, 'I have an acquaintance. For the sake of tact, let us call her Frau X. Now Frau X – who is as good a woman as you or I, I assure you – does not believe that the poor are indeed poor. "They do not look undernourished," she says, "like they used to."' Polster had caught the self-satisfied tone of the 'acquaintance' to perfection, and a rustle of indignation spread through the hall. Lilli felt it in herself too – the shame and the recoil, the rapid relief when a scapegoat was offered – felt it just for a moment before she realised that she had been manipulated, and that Frau Polster only had to conjure up the spectre of a cold-hearted woman and she had the entire audience exactly where she wanted them. Lilli leaned forward, angry now, straining to hear.

'Frau X who would prefer the poor to be both starving and meek, who would never in a hundred years force herself to do what I and my sisters have done so many times . . . to step inside the dark tenements and see the black grease on the cookers, see the child on a heap of grey blankets spreading margarine with his fingers on a piece of half-gnawed bread . . .'

From the row behind Lilli came a low sigh, and then a sob, quickly stifled. Frau Polster raised her eyes to the gallery and nodded majestically. 'Sisters. I realise that what I have to say may well shock some of you. Together we have fought hunger and want, we have fought the despair which stems from poverty and eats at the heart of the nation. But there is another enemy to fight, believe me. Some of you who visit regularly at the houses of the poor will not have failed to notice the overcrowded conditions in which brother must sleep with sister, and father with daughter. The beds where three, four, half a dozen children huddle together for warmth. Nor will you have failed to notice girls fallen pregnant on the mere threshold of maturity, and wondered deep in yourselves at this collapse of the normal standards of decency . . .'

Lilli stared at the programme in her lap. *The Silver Mountain*, she read for the tenth time: *a film by Thea Holstein*. She had shredded a small even frill around the edge. 'I used to know her,' she'd told Frau Kessel in an unguarded moment. Excitement fluttering under her ribs. 'Not well,' she'd lied hastily, seeing the fund-raising fervour glint in Frau Kessel's eyes. 'I'm sure she wouldn't remember me.'

On the platform Frau Polster was working up to a resounding finish. 'Sisters,' she thundered. 'I entreat you. Look into your hearts and ask yourselves if you can remain mere bystanders, or whether with me you will become crusaders to remove this moral taint from our nation!' Turning on her heel, Frau Polster left the stage abruptly; the applause echoed to the rafters, calling her back and back.

'What a woman,' said Frau Kessel, turning a glowing face on Lilli. 'What an inspiration!'

Lilli nodded grimly. For a *Narzisse*, she thought. Had she said as much, Frau Kessel would have been hurt, her kind heart affronted. 'There are good women in all camps,' she would have said reproachfully. 'I've always believed that is our salvation.' When Frau Kessel was in the full flush of enthusiasm it was useless to argue with her.

On the platform a vote of thanks was asked for and given, and then suddenly there was Thea, hatless and trousered, striding into the light. Catching her breath, Lilli craned forward. Saw Thea bow low to the welcoming applause, saw how her hair – no longer dark now, but a light straw-gold cut in a loose bob to the shoulder – swung glittering into her eyes. Gaped, too, at the crocodile-skin shoes, the suave cut of the dark green jacket and slacks. Staring so, Lilli even fancied for a moment that Thea had glimpsed her, and had to remind herself that Thea, blinded by the spotlight, could see nothing: even if she were to stand up and wave her red hat wildly she would be no more than a blur at the back of the gallery.

Thea murmured obligatory words: so privileged to appear, there are some causes one can't refuse, etcetera etcetera. As the house lights dimmed and the projector in the aisle of the gallery began to whirr Lilli clasped her hands tightly in her lap and tried to compose herself, but already her mind was leafing backwards through the years, the black dates stripping off the calendar faster than any American film: Thea in the room above the grocery store, draped in a dark green curtain; one shoulder bare, a raddled silk scarf for a turban, and the moon high and white behind her. Cushions were piled by the open window where her father's telescope, steeply angled, pointed up over the rooftops of the town. A cold wind blew in through the window as Thea, goosepimpling, put her eye to the lens. *Look Lilli, look. It's beginning*! Through the telescope the night sky was blue as day, the moon impossibly high and sailing. And then a shadow narrowed it, a chunk had been bitten out . . . and Thea was laughing and crying, thumping her head into the cushions, her turban dislodged and her dark hair everywhere, drunk, feverish, transported. *Ah Lilli, Lilli, how lovely*!

For it was. Yes. The film which had flickered and taken shape on the screen in the Town Hall *was* lovely. Lovely the shadows of the birch branches wavering on Marta's ragged dress as she raised her eyes to the silver mountain; lovely the full moon rising behind its glittering summit. Ugly, by contrast, the sanctimonious church-goers, the usurers in the market-place, the card-sharps in the inn. Ugly the bitter faces of the village women who dragged their sons indoors at sunset so that the dangerous enchantment of the full moon could not draw them towards the terrible heights. Only Marta, it was clear – Marta the wild, Marta the chaste, Marta the outcast – only Marta might dare the rock precipices, might penetrate the silver grotto and kneel (oh Thea!) haloed in purity, her lithe body silhouetted against the light.

Watching, Lilli's head began to ache, and her mind raced to and fro in pursuit of an indefinable alarm. For Thea the actress was one thing, but Thea the director was quite another. And what on earth was this new Thea saying? That Marta, unlike the villagers, was untainted by materialistic desires or the petty imperatives of religion? Incarnated, perhaps, some pagan spirit which they had cast out of their lives? So that when the village men brought ladders and picks to exploit the precious silver and desecrate the womb of the mountain, Marta too was desecrated, and the only dénouement was death, chilly, the final freeze-frame: Thea's lovely body fallen from the heights and sprawled heroically among flowers.

When the lights went up and the spell was broken Lilli's alarm was replaced by a dull embarrassment at Thea's excesses. Oh Thea, she thought, shaking her head at this Marta who excited fear, envy, lust, but did not feel them; this Marta who glittered monthly under the full moon but did not bleed. This Marta who would not surrender to a real lover, but only to some higher necessity — to Fate or Destiny or the pure will of the mountain and all its frozen edges. Certainly, Lilli enjoyed a fairytale as much as anyone, had been stirred, she admitted it, mesmerised in her simple-minded self, couldn't help thrilling to the omnipotence of it all, the dream and the swoon . . . but oh Thea, she thought. Oh Thea, what frigid, narcissistic tosh!

When Lilli stood up to leave, the Party stalwarts in their little brown blouses and little blue skirts were still applauding wildly. At the exit she brushed two of them aside, frowning at their newsletters and their sharp scrubbed faces, and caught sight of Thea in the foyer, surrounded by autograph books. Thea was smiling intently at each signee, stooping to envelop each one in a momentary, glamorous intimacy. In the face of such practised charm Lilli hung back, her confidence flagging. Since she could not honestly say that she had liked the film, she would probably say nothing at all, would be reduced — by her own ambivalence, if not by Thea's overpowering presence — to a dumb, smiling discomfiture. Or so she reasoned as she stood rooted to the spot in the hubbub, until finally the indomitable Frau Kessel sailed into the fray, towing Lilli in her wake.

Later, dwelling on the reunion, Lilli remembered how Thea had caught sight of her as she was being propelled through the crowd, and had blinked her eyes wide, twice, in a mannerism which left the moony whites suddenly too bulbous and exposed, a mannerism which Lilli had forgotten. 'Darling Lilli,' she cried, 'Is it really you?' Lilli introduced Frau Kessel, who talked breathlessly about the Hospital Fund for a few moments and then, pressing Thea's hand, sallied off in search of the *Bankhaus* Meusel. And then somewhow Lilli and Thea had pushed their way through the glass doors and were out on the bustle of Marienplatz, leaving the clamorous crowd behind them.

Lilli giggled. 'Your nose,' she said, shooting glances at an altered profile.

'Ssh,' said Thea, tucking Lilli's arm through hers. 'In Hollywood the plastic surgeon takes over where the Almighty gave up in despair! But yes, I've remade myself – hair, everything.' America was a madhouse, she told Lilli, thanking God she was home to stay, gaily, talking hell for leather, steering Lilli across the street between lit and clanking trams to a café terrace overhung by walnut trees, and so accustomed was Lilli to Thea's taking the initiative, so easily did she fall back into the old ways, that it hardly occurred to her to protest that in Munich she, rather than Thea, should properly play host.

Thea chose a table on the terrace and sniffed avidly. How she'd missed the smells, she said. More than anything she'd missed the smells. Roast almonds. Bitter chocolate. 'But you, Lilli? Are you married? Lovers? Children? I have to know everything, you see!'

At a nearby table a young woman licked her finger with a laugh and removed a rim of coffee froth from her lover's upper lip, while, tethered to her chair leg, a terrier with a bandaged paw panted adoringly up at her. Watching them, Lilli was sad, suddenly, and didn't want to be: after all, she could honestly say that she hardly had time to be lonely. 'I'm a workhorse at the moment,' she confessed, 'until my training finishes.'

'Like me, darling,' sighed Thea. 'Like me.'

Lilli was surprised, and said so. She couldn't imagine a solitary Thea, a Thea without swains. 'But didn't you marry an industrialist? I read it in the newspapers.'

'Yes, and I can't tell you how hard it was keeping up a sane conversation about machine tools!' Thea threw back her head and laughed voluptuously, her face radiant, her hair swinging in a blonde sheet. 'Oh Lilli, I never was cut out for marriage, was I?' And people on the terrace turned their heads to look, and the waiter smiled as he set their drinks on the table, and as Lilli clinked her glass against Thea's she saw again the threadbare room above the grocery, and Thea stretched out across the cushions, grand as Cleopatra, brandishing, at fourteen, a bottle of Tokay stolen from the rack in the cellar: *No more* Knodelfrauen, *Lilli. And no babies to hang on our skirts*!

Pure will power, Lilli thought. That's what Thea had, and perhaps that's what you needed when you hadn't had much of a start. When the stairs were narrow and leaning and the carpets quite worn out, and you had to go each day to the *Bürgerschule* with a slate in your satchel — only at the *Hohere Tochterschule* did they have real copybooks — and the ubiquitous sponge which dangled from its string. The sponge which, far from wiping anything out, announced in capital letters that you'd come down in the world. No wonder, then, that Thea swore she would get out, toasted them both in Tokay, stolen and golden. They would be free and fine and famous, not trapped, like the *Hausfrau*s of the village, not *dumplingwomen*, milk-stained and miserable. Words floated back to Lilli. A remark her mother had made about Thea. *That girl's so envious, she'd steal your very death*. One of her odd things, overheard murmurs from the bedroom. Like: *Lilli's not a jealous girl, look how good she is to her little sisters.* Eavesdropping, Lilli had wanted to cry out that it wasn't true, that she was bad, bad as Thea or worse, but somehow the words refused to move from her mind to her mouth and in her tongue-tied tangle she was duty bound to cherish Thea more than ever, her loyalty fervent and illicit as a furled flag.

'Ach but Lilli,' Thea shrugged. 'Men are so useless nowadays. They whine, they're like fatherless children.' She brought out a silver cigarette case and offered it, lighting one for herself. She waved a casual hand but her eyes were on Lilli, pale green and penetrating. 'They need a strong man to put them back in order, no?'

For a moment Lilli couldn't speak. She picked up the cigarette case and turned it over in her hands. Inside, an elastic band held in place a rank of smooth white cylinders, neat as invalids in a hospital ward. She had gone to one of the rallies once, had stood at the back in a straggle of sceptics and social democrats, listening to the orations. A man she'd recognised as one of the Hospital porters had spat on the ground and was hustled out by the brown-shirted guards, cursing. She had left then, but she'd already seen enough. She closed the cigarette case with a snap. 'Last week, Thea, I was in a café with Frau Kessel. And there was a couple, quite like that couple there, the ones with the dog. Only they weren't laughing, Thea, they were quiet, and held hands. There was a rose on the table, a rose he had given her. And then two SA men came in and sat down on either side of them, so that the four of them were in a line, shoulder to shoulder, although there were plenty of empty seats on the terrace. And one of the SA picked up the rose and began to pull the petals off one by one — he loves me, he loves me not, remember? Until the petals were all shredded on the ground.' Lilli's voice trembled, remembering the silence that had fallen, the hastily averted eyes. 'And no one moved a muscle, Thea. Because the boy and girl were Jewish, you see.'

A frenzied yelping broke out at the neighbouring table. The terrier, which had tangled its injured paw in the leash, was untied and picked up and petted. Thea stared distantly at the spectacle, her eyes narrowed. 'Forgive me, Lilli, but sometimes you have to be realistic.'

'Oh I am, Thea!' Lilli heard her voice rise in sarcasm. 'Frau Kessel is the rash one, not me. I think she might have attacked them with her umbrella if I hadn't dragged her bodily on to the *Strassenbahn*.' Suddenly her eyes were full of tears.

'Darling bravest Lilli.' Thea patted Lilli's hand, the fingers fluttering over hers and settling. 'You always did take things so hard.'

Strings of coloured lights winked in the walnut trees, tinkling against one another when a wind stirred the branches. Out on the square the pavements were crowded and the department store windows glittered in anticipation of Christmas. Lilli shook her head fiercely, pushing away her old self: Lilli the over-sensitive, the shedder of helpless tears. 'Terrible things are happening, Thea,' she accused.

Thea frowned. Her fingers were long and pale, playing in the dark fox fur of her collar. 'You think I don't know that?'

'I'm sorry, Thea, but I thought . . .' Thea was staring, and Lilli stammered to a halt.

'For God's sake, Lilli, I'm no Nazi, if that's what you mean!' Thea gave a short laugh, shocked. Lilli's face flamed. She sat in confusion, shaking her head. Yes, that had been her implication, she couldn't deny it. But then she saw that

Thea was smiling. As Lilli watched, Thea's features wavered wickedly, shifted, and finally settled into a mould which was so gimlet-eyed and purse-lipped, so unmistakably Polster, that she put her head in her hands and burst into horrified laughter.

'I should think so too!' cried Thea, egging Lilli on with a merry energy that put her doubts to shame – (Thea who could, as always, be for you whatever you wanted her to be, Thea who pulled out a chequebook and dashed off a cheque for Frau Kessel, Thea who reminded you teasingly of the Art Class in '15, when you were required to paint a battle scene and painted instead a Red Cross tent with German soldiers bandaged up like mummies. Emmy Debus had put up her hand and told the teacher that you must be a traitor, because only English soldiers got killed, everybody knew that, and the class had jeered at you until, bursting into sobs, you cried out: If only English soldiers get killed, then why did Thea's father?).

'So you see, Lilli, you were *always* brave!' said Thea, Thea who blew daintily into her leather gloves and wriggled her fingers inside, Thea who planted a smacking kiss first on one cheek and then the other, and holding Lilli at arms' length made her promise that should she ever need her, she mustn't hesitate . . . stopping Lilli's protest with her hand – 'Darling, I can *afford* it' – the leather damp and cool against Lilli's mouth. Then she straightened, touched the tip of Lilli's nose with her forefinger, turned in a flurry of fur, waved once, and strode away across the terrace, her chameleon hair lit red and blue and green under the shifting lights.

1991, MINNA

Of all media, film is perhaps the most innocent. We take them on trust, these characters without pasts who appear in front of us and, moving through a seamless succession of presents, vindicate or betray themselves by their actions alone, without the usual recourse to excuses, memories, analysis, so that when we judge them — as we do, the role of jury being the one assigned to us — we look in vain for extenuating circumstances which might mitigate our verdict.

Austria. Fire and ice. The insatiable eye of Thea's camera on the Nesthorn. In the Film Archive they tell me that, apart from *The Silver Mountain*, most of the early films were destroyed in the bombardments. Of the later works, *Shadows on the Snow* — made in 1945, just before the war was lost — remains, although one reel is missing, and on the others some sequences are partly or wholly obliterated, the celluloid flickering with white scratches like a scarred cornea.

> *Fade in on*: A girl with chestnut hair walking up a forest path, leaves and flowers woven into her hair, Ophelia-like. Peaks painted or not crane in the distance, and cloud shadows seem to move on them (although this effect may be attributable to the accidental flickering of a projector bulb or a stray wisp of smoke from the projectionist's cigarette).
> *Cut to*: The girl emerging from the forest and stopping on a precipitous bluff. Hallooing. Cowbells tinkle on the soundtrack as a farmer harvesting hay in a field far below looks up and waves. But now a thrown pine cone startles the girl, and there's a giggle, glimpse of a sunburned face upside down, knees flashing as the owner uncurls from a

branch and jumps down. A hat with a small feather, breeches – but it's a girl who's in them, a blonde girl who kisses her friend on both cheeks and leads her up the zigzagging path until at last she stops and, tying a scarf over her friend's eyes, turns her by the shoulders, spins her once, twice, three times. *Look*, she cries, pulling the scarf away.

Cut to: A mountain hut built of rough logs. Moss grows on the dilapidated roof-tiles and a chimney pot sits askew. Red-haired Elsa is hesitant as blonde Magda boldly prises the upper latch open and slips her hand inside to unbolt the lower door. *Dare we?*

Cut to interior: Elsa bustles with dusting rags and sweeping brush and soon a fire has been lit in the pot-bellied stove and a jar of Alpine flowers set on the table. *We'll milk the goats and fetch fresh eggs from the farmer*, says Elsa. Magda holds up a heavy iron key, triumphant. *And we'll never have to go back down to the village again*! But now Magda stops dead, a finger to her lips.

Cut to: The open doorway. A bird's egg flies through the door and breaks open at Elsa's feet. A dead gosling is curled inside, streaked with yolk and blood. Elsa kneels down and cradles the small corpse in her lap, staining her white dress with blood. Her hair is illuminated by a shaft of sunlight. A tear runs down her cheek. But now a shadow blots out the gentle shaft of light: a huge shadow, angular, hands on its hips. Whirling round, Magda seizes the alpenstock which stands by the fireplace.

Cut to: A boy of about sixteen, standing in the doorway with two cronies leering behind him. His trousers are patched and torn and his dirty gypsy face is twisted into lines of cruelty and cunning. He grasps a lock of Elsa's hair and coils it round his finger with a terrible smile. But now Magda springs at him, lashing out with the alpenstock. Bleeding from the forehead, the bully blusters and threatens, until at last his cronies drag him away.

Here the film deteriorates. Shadows loom at the edges and eventually occlude the entire frame, and the projectionist takes the remaining reel from its heavy aluminium can.

Close up: Magda, some years older, is stretched out in a sunny meadow. Her hair is bobbed and her skirts mid-calf, as befits a young lady at the *Gymnasium*. Wind stirs the pages of the book at which she glances from time to time as she waits for Elsa. The shadow of the mountain is lengthening and still Elsa has not arrived, and Magda's face grows worried. Shielding her eyes against the sun she squints up at the precipitous bluff. She sees tiny figures moving slowly on the forest path. One of the figures, in white, is being dragged, hauled along like a sack of potatoes.
Cut to: The village. Loutish faces peer from the dark doorway of an inn.
Cut to: A narrow street where a drunk man and woman abuse each other. Magda races through the streets, crosses the river bridge where water torrents, and gains at last the safety of a white house surrounded by two hedges, the outer of hawthorn and the inner of cyclamen.
Cut to: Magda's bedroom. Magda tears off the ladylike dress and dons her old breeches.
Cut to: Magda's father's study. Close up on a photograph on the desk – Magda's father as a young officer in the uniform of the Kaiser's army, medals on his breast.
Pan to: The door of the study, which bursts open. Magda enters, runs to a heavy oak chest and pulls out her father's pistol.

Cut to: The doorway, where Magda's mother stands, hands on hips, aproned and forbidding.
Cut to: Magda standing next to the photograph of her father, defiant, clutching the pistol to her breast.
Flashback to: The sunlight striking Elsa's hair as she knelt all that time ago on the floor of the mountain hut, and then the angular shadow blotting the light out.
Cut to: The good Frau, who flings her arms wide to block Magda's way, entreating her. Magda thrusts her aside.
Cut to: Magda running through the meadow and stopping at the bottom of the precipice. Thrusting the pistol into her belt she flings herself at the sheer rock face and begins to climb, ropeless, and fast, and perilous, unleashing small avalanches of pebbles, poised above the sickening drop for a moment and then moving on again, delicate as a dragonfly, profiled against the sky until at last her strong hands grip the lip of the precipice and she heaves herself up and over.
Cut to: The hut in the forest clearing. The door is bolted and barred, and Magda creeps to the shuttered window.
Close up: on Magda, her eye to a crack in the shutter.
Cut to: Interior. Elsa is huddled on a truckle bed in the corner, weeping.
Cut to: Elsa's POV as the twisted face of the ruffian leans over her.
Cut to: Magda wrenching open the shutters, firing. Light streams into the room as Elsa's tormentor falls, light full on his bleeding face, his eyes wide open in surprise.
Music now: The ending. The cohorts have fled and Magda kneels by the bed, stroking Elsa's long chestnut hair.
Forgive me, she murmurs – tantalisingly, implying some previous quarrel, separation, betrayal, some transgression depicted elsewhere, on the lost reel perhaps, on the reel

that's missing. *Forgive me, Elsa*, as Elsa throws her arms round her friend, as the camera
Cuts to: An exterior shot of the rough mountain hut in the forest glade,
Pans across the wooded valley
Rises to focus on the very summits of the snow-capped mountains, settles there as
The Credits climb the screen.

1940, LILLI

By the winter of '39, Franz said, he and Lilli had been together for a year, at first working side by side at the hospital, later sleeping at each other's apartments, making plans which were only partly the plans of lovers.

When Lilli drew the blackout curtains aside the January sun glinted on the mirror above the washstand, dazzling her. Franz was wrestling with his collar studs, his neck stretched out, his chin scraped clean of hairs and jutting sharply. He was recounting, as he did every morning, last night's dreams.

'So then a man comes into the room,' he said. 'It's afternoon, but the blinds are down and the bedcovers are rumpled. Then the man's hand goes down on to the bed and he feels the damp patch with a blank, dreamy look in his eyes. There's wet on his fingers and he's staring at them, but he still won't let himself believe what his eyes tell him. He won't let himself see that his wife's having an affair . . .' Franz caught Lilli's eye in the mirror and winked. 'Maybe I'm afraid Father will fall in love with you. He always did have a yen for the New Woman!'

Lilli's reflection frowned back at her from the mirror: the

narrow face under the fox-red brush of hair, the apprehensive expression around the eyes which in a younger woman might have suggested an appealing timidity, but which nowadays, she'd decided, only succeeded in making her look sly. 'Shouldn't you be more afraid that I'll fall in love with him?'

'Well, he gets *crushes*, you know.' Franz's face was comically puritanical.

'Terrible Oedipal boy,' Lilli retorted, jabbing a comb into her hair and pushing the red curls up and forward to frame her face. Irritably, for if Franz shared her qualms about the meeting with his father he was concealing it all too well, teasing her while she trembled. 'Better that he does get a crush! Given the situation.'

Franz had stretched out on the bed and lay there with his arms folded behind his head, watching her dress. 'Know why Hitler walks around with his hands clasped across his belly? He's protecting the last unemployed member of the Reich.' Franz guffawed at the old joke, beating his heels uproariously against the bed until the springs jangled and the small room shuddered like a ferryboat in a gale. '*Courage*, my Lilli!' he cried, crossing the room in one bound, arms held wide to embrace her, romping at her like some great boy just let out of school.

'Anyone would think you were looking forward to this,' Lilli said sourly, plucking his watch from the washstand and thrusting it into his waistcoat pocket.

'All the same,' Franz said with a sigh. 'About the Clinic plan. It would be better if you didn't mention too many Jewish names. No, don't argue. I know you. Once you start talking about your precious children you forget yourself.'

Lilli protested then, and vehemently: to ask Herr Müller for money yet keep him in ignorance was immoral, she argued, and Franz argued back. He was tall and thin and towered above her, hands on her shoulders, persuading her.

'Just remember he's a pragmatist, Lilli, for all his Prussian honour. And believe me, there are some things he'd rather not know.'

'So pretty, Fräulein, and not married yet?'

Confronted not by the elderly Prussian gentleman she had expected, but by this elegant widower whose glance – for all his gallant manners – was cool and astute, Lilli flushed and looked away. *My colleague*, Franz had called her, but had Herr Müller been in the slightest bit deceived? The floor of the semi-circular conservatory was tiled in pale ceramic, and the upright chairs were starkly scarlet: it was all so admirably modern, this room without pouffes or tassels or the comforting gloom of chenille curtains, this light and gleaming room which branded her as a liar.

Franz was hovering behind her, hands on the back of her chair. 'The Hospital is a State concern now, Father. Lilli would have to resign if she married.'

'Do sit down, Franz,' sighed Herr Müller. 'I'm quite capable of grasping the laws of the land without your reminders.' Frowning judiciously, he tapped out an English cigarette in a square glass ashtray. 'A forthright man, your Herr Kessel, and a fine doctor. I don't see that Germany can be anything but poorer for the loss of such people.'

With perfect sang-froid Herr Müller had summed up his position, and now he was all charm again, his beaming blue gaze holding her. Balanced on the inhospitable chair, Lilli found herself nodding. Case dismissed, she thought. Just as Frau Kessel's had been, despite the mountain of paper which moved back and forth between the Ministry of Justice and the Maximilianstrasse – certificates of baptism, affidavits, testimonials pleading two Aryan grandparents and a

Catholic father – but even then Frau Kessel had refused to see the writing on the wall. It had taken weeks of persuasion – Lilli and the Herr Doktor in accord for once – before Frau Kessel would consent to uprooting husband and home and starting afresh in America.

'But Fräulein Kirchner, you were telling me about Lindau. A pretty place, as I recall. Always had a notion to try this water-skiing they do down on the Bodensee. You've seen suitable premises, I take it?'

Lilli set her cup carefully back in its saucer and described the hotel above the lake – not large, but perfect for their purposes. 'The owners recently . . . emigrated,' Franz added.

Herr Müller brushed away the euphemism impatiently. And the price, he pressed, was it reasonable?

Oh, very, Lilli thought bitterly. Prices were these days. Less reasonable, on the other hand, for the expropriated. Sweat broke out on her upper lip as Franz regaled his father with figures: income, expenditure, annual shortfall. Herr Müller was jotting down calculations in a small black notebook. Gripping her bag in both hands she looked him straight in the eye and willed him to believe in her. 'We can do valuable work, Herr Müller. I can't tell you how valuable.'

1943, MINNA

Dear Lilli and Uncle Franz,

This is a drawing of a fiter plane, it is an Ally plane with red and blue circles. The plane cant fly because the injin is brocken. Uri has a boil on his nose and on Saturday we saw a big avalansh on the mountain and he cryed. I wish you were here to go tobogning with Uri and me. Tante

Freda is learning us words of Englisch like yes please and excuse me to be polite.
Love and XXXX from Minna

Dear Lilli,
In Engeland people play monopli, you can buy stashuns and have a metal boot but I dont like it to play because Englisch numbers are funny and London was all dark and we were fritened. Tante Hanna says the Red Cross will bring you this scarf I nitted for Christmas. Here it is diffrent dinner not carp with things in it but puding with sixpennys. I hope you have lots of presints and Uncle Franz too. Tante Hanna says we can rite letters to Santa Claus like children do in London and send them up the chimny, Uncle Franz sent us transfers to stick in our schoolbooks. Uri askt for a fish like Albert in the tank but Tante Hanna says you cant rite just now. Uri plays tunels in the yard, he says you can dig a tunel to escape like Englisch prisoners do from Hitler, he crys every nite.
With Happy Christmas from Minna.

1991, MINNA

What I do remember is the fish, Lilli. Such a northern, bluish, mackerel-like fish, incongruous among those others, those tropical ones with their fins which wavered like petals in the greenish water of the tank. And I see Uri press his mouth to the glass close to where the mouth of the fish pulsated. 'See, Lilli, he's kissing me!' he cried, mimicking, his lips smacking noisily, and if you pulled him away then, sharply, like a harassed mother, perhaps it was because you had already prepared too many children for separations, had stuffed bread and sausage into their pockets and sent them across the border to invented parents, little false families with false papers, some of whom could be relied upon to remember their new names, others, like Käthe and poor demented Jacob, firmly enjoined to silence.

And perhaps it's because the harshness was so uncharacteristic of you that the memory persists: Uri's lips glued to the glass and the kiss until he is torn away bodily (did he already know without knowing, as children do, that we would be gone within the week?). So that when Thea was shown into the library he recoiled in tears from this red-lipped stranger who asked the names of the fish and bent down to comfort him, and running instead to you he clung pitifully to your skirts, alternately rubbing his tears away with his fist and aiming childish punches at Thea, until at last you begged me to take him out of the room so that you could properly attend to your glamorous guest.

It was from the kitchen window, while Uri drank milk and muttered to himself, that I watched you walk on the terrace with Thea — jealously, watched and judged, for it was a dumb show I didn't understand. You were pointing to the other side of the lake, you were pointing to Switzerland, you were standing by the balustrade with the print of Thea's lipstick still on your cheek and her hand possessive over yours. Your face in the full sunlight was soft with gratitude, while a few feet away Franz smoked a cigarette in the shadow of the yew tree, frowning and wary, as well he might have been, for it was 1942, the dark heart of the War, and so many upright citizens would have seen it as their bounden duty to betray you.

1991, ILSE

Lilli Kirchner? A psychoanalyst? No, I can't say I've ever heard the name. Certainly not from Frau Holstein. Perhaps a childhood friend? Oh yes, Frau Holstein was very clear in her mind, right up to the day she died. I'm no women's libber, but that's often the way, you know, with ladies who've led an active life, rather than those who, well, their children leave and their husband dies and there they sit in their big empty houses with their silverware and their walnut whatnots, and they just go to pieces, poor dears . . . Yes, indeed it was a tragedy, for Frau Holstein to be struck down in her prime, and especially with the profession she was in. It was the Gestapo torture, you know, that blinded her. Dreadful. Those animals. Beg pardon? Who told me? Well, I'm not exactly sure, now you come to mention it. I thought it was common knowledge. I must have heard it from Frau Holstein herself, I suppose. Not that she was one for making a song and dance about what's past and done with. I believe she even mentioned the July plot of '44, although you'll be a bit young to remember that, I imagine. Oh, you were brought up in England? Well, you have very good German if you don't mind my saying. Yes, it's true that Frau Holstein moved in the highest circles but so did some of the conspirators and that didn't save them, did it?

But Frau Holstein was a woman without bitterness. Never played the martyr, as many would have, although how she could forgive those rascals after what they did to her is beyond me. At least my conscience is clear, Ilse, she used to say, just think what they have to live with.

. . . The Müller Clinic? It wasn't on the corniche road above Meersburg, was it? I can't say it rings a bell, although of course I was very young myself then, little more than a girl . . . It's quite possible that there was a special sanatorium for children round here; in this region you can't move for sanatoria, as my husband Otto used to say – he worked in the Rheumatology Institute himself, up at Oberreitnau.

. . . since 1960 or, let me see, it must have been 1961 when I took the engagement with Frau Holstein. Well, it's odd you should say so, because we watched it together on the television. We watched it go up, and then last year, just before she died, we watched it come down again. Frau Holstein made me tell her every last detail, all these young – what do you call them in English? Ah, punks also? – all these young punks tearing at the concrete with their bare hands. And although Frau Holstein wasn't one for showing her feelings I could see that she was moved in herself. I remember we even drank a glass of champagne together, because although it was right that Germany had to be punished for, well, all the bad things, of course, Frau Holstein was a patriot, you understand, and none of us ordinary folk ever wanted to see our country cut in half.

. . . Beg pardon? The view from the terrace? Yes, it *is* very pretty, isn't it, with the lake and the Swiss mountains. Just like a picture-book, my Otto used to say.

For Nature has placed inside women's bodies in a secret intestinal place an animal, *a member, which is not in man, in which sometimes are engendered certain saline, nitrous, boracic, acrid, biting, shooting, bitterly tickling humors, through whose prickling and grievous wriggling (for this member is very nervous and sensitive) the entire body is shaken, all the senses ravished, all inclinations unleashed, all thoughts confounded . . .*

François Rabelais, *The Heroic Deeds and Sayings of the Good Pantagruel*, Book III, chapter xxxii (1584)

The Photographer . . . needs in many cases no aid from any language of his own, but prefers rather to listen, with the picture before him, to the silent but telling language of nature — It is unnecessary for him to use the vague terms which denote a difference in the degree of mental suffering, as for instance, distress, sorrow, deep sorrow, grief, melancholy, anguish, despair; the picture speaks for itself with the most marked pression and indicates the exact point which has been reached in the scale of unhappiness between the first sensation and its utmost height . . .

Hugh W. Diamond, *On the Application of Photography to the Physiognomic and Mental Phenomena of Insanity*

Read before the Royal Society, 22 May 1856

DYSPLASIA

Leslie Dick

a malady through representation

It was always unclear whether there was something wrong with her, or not.

The woman said the cervix looked lacerated. She asked Gina if she had had an abortion. Gina hadn't, then. The woman said, because your cervix looks lacerated. Then she said, deformed.

So it was never very clear whether there was something wrong with her, or not. Something looked wrong, clearly. That woman had called in another doctor, an older woman, who took one look (Gina lying flat, the speculum inserted) and said, D-E-S. It was the first time Gina'd heard of it. Gina was nineteen.

She wrote a letter to her mother in Paris, and her mother wrote back. Yes, she'd taken it, she said she'd taken it, this drug, diethylstilboestrol, she'd taken it throughout her pregnancy with Gina. The drug was meant to prevent miscarriage; that's why her mother took it. The doctors stopped prescribing it to pregnant women some time in the 1960s. It was known to cause malformations of the cervix and vagina; it was known to cause cancer; no one knew what else it did. Thus Gina found herself one of a group, a group of daughters, women who apparently had something wrong with them, maybe.

No other doctor, and there were many of them over the years, peering up into her inner recesses, her nether cavities, her cunt, no other doctor ever exclaimed at the sight of her cervix quite like that. Sometimes Gina wondered if the woman had been exaggerating. Was it simply that the other doctors were more guarded, or tactful? Better trained to deal with this monstrosity? Lacerated. Deformed. Or maybe they didn't notice, maybe there was really nothing to see.

Gina looked it up in the dictionary. The chemical formula was asymmetric, like her cervix: $OHC_6H_4CH{:}CHC_6H_4OH$.

There was nothing (seriously) wrong with her. There was nothing wrong with her.

hysterosalpingogram

What do I remember? It's so hard to say. I remember this doctor in Chicago, this woman doctor, saying to me, 'Well, I'm sorry to have to tell you this, but with your history, you will have grave fertility problems.'

I liked her, this woman doctor, but I found it exhausting: having to take all these drugs, all this fucking metronidazole, and doxycyclin, and at the same time, having to take in the idea of 'grave fertility problems' as some kind of inevitability. My very own scarred Fallopian tubes.

And then there's the cancer stuff. I have to have these regular special cancer tests or investigations, scrutinies really, they scrutinize my interior, the doctors, anyway I have to have them at regular intervals because my mother took this drug when she was pregnant with me. It seeped through her placenta, like poison. It was meant to prevent miscarriage, and as she always says, I was the most wanted baby in the world. Most wanted, like a criminal, I always think. Anyway the drug makes me susceptible to a form of cancer that never existed before, a form of cancer that apparently is only found in the female children of women who took diethylstilboestrol during pregnancy. The threatened cancer is cancer of the vagina, which is relatively dire, because when it happens they have to more or less take your vagina out. You become like a sex change person, someone with a little hollow instead of a vagina, a little concavity to signify the possibility of penetration, or femininity, or something.

I suppose by that time you're glad you're still alive. Apparently this horrorshow is not very likely to happen to me though, because it seems to take place before you're twenty, if it's going to happen at all. On the other hand, we're all under fifty, us DES daughters, so they really don't know what's going to happen to us as we get older. That's the reason to keep an eye on us, give us regular colposcopies.

A colposcopy is like this: you lie on your back on a table with your legs drawn up, like an ordinary exam, but the table rises up hydraulically, so that the doctor sitting comfortably at the end of the table is looking directly into your vagina. Your cunt is at his eye level, in other words. He inserts a speculum, and then a kind of microscope, so that the cells of the vaginal wall are seen in extreme close up. Usually there is a big black Nikormat camera attached to the colposcope, in case they see anything worth photographing, and the doctor sits down comfortably and looks into you through two eye-pieces, just like binoculars. There is a third eye-piece, like a long thin telescope, that comes out of the top of the colposcope apparatus, allowing a third person to stand next to the seated doctor and peer into the inner recesses also. It's quite amusing, reminiscent of Jules Verne somehow, submarines.

Then he takes a bit of cotton wool and dips it in vinegar, and paints that on the walls of the vagina, all the while expressing doubt that you are in fact a DES baby. He looks at the effects of the vinegar and becomes even more vehement. 'There is no sign of any abnormality,' he says. I go on lying there, having been through this movie before. Whereupon he does the second test, which is to paint the vagina with iodine. Suddenly there's great excitement: a result. He says, 'Well, well, well,' very quickly, and calls his colleague over, who rushes up to peer into the telescope, as the first doctor frantically describes what they're both seeing. It's all Greek to me. The doctor looks up over my belly and says, 'This is textbook stuff, very good, we must get it on video next time!' He's thrilled. I'm pleased when, having accepted that I am indeed one of these DES cases, they have a good look at my weird cells and decide I don't have cancer, for the time being. I'm allowed to get dressed, to go home.

In the office, the doctor rubs his hands together and says, 'Right! We'll see you again in what — six months? That's a bit soon, isn't it? Let's say nine months — six is too short, twelve is too long! Let's say nine!' I say, all right.

Thus every nine months, instead of giving birth to a baby, I go and have my cancer test. It's always a bit nerve-wracking; I'm terrified they'll tell me I've got cancer, needless to say. But they are very nice to me, and quite often they invite visitors, spectators, so to speak, to look at my special effects, to see how the vinegar does nothing, but one mustn't be downcast, because the iodine performs like fireworks in there. Watch.

The last time, last year, I saw this very nice woman who

had previously been the sort of second in command, the one standing over the spyglass, peering in with one eye screwed shut. She seemed to be Italian, originally, and she did the whole vinegar and iodine routine, during which I'm lying there, fingers crossed, and then she said, 'I don't like what I see.' I went into shock. Then she said, 'But I think you should come back and see the consultant. I'm really a fertility specialist, not a cancer specialist, and I can't really tell what I'm looking at.' I was surprised and really very pleased: most doctors don't let on when they don't know what they're doing. As I got dressed I told her some of my fertility anxieties: how this doctor in Chicago had said that my tubes were maybe blocked, how I'd had this infection and that disease, and I was worried because I wanted to have a baby, sometime. She said, 'I can refer you to my fertility clinic, here's the number, give us a call and make an appointment.' I was pleased, despite the cancer stuff.

So I had to come back and see the Great Man Himself. His name was Dr Savage, if you can believe it. But he was terribly busy, or something, so I had to wait a couple of weeks before I could see him. I was quite scared. When I finally went for my appointment, I almost went to the wrong hospital. I quite often make slips like that with my cancer tests, I go to Gower Street instead of Goodge Street, and then I have to run, not to be late. Anyway, there were hordes of spectators this time, like five people (mostly men) in this little room, and most surprising of all, right beside me as I reclined on the examination table, was a massive, 24-inch Sony Trinitron video monitor, which seemed to be attached to a little video camera that was going to be aimed into my vagina.

The TV set was about three inches away from me, conveniently angled so that the doctor performing the colposcopy could see the magnified image on the TV screen, rather than having to look through the binoculars. I was quite excited: I'd never seen my cervix on TV before. When it appeared on the screen, I was completely surprised. It didn't look the way I expected it to at all. The colours were truly lurid: livid greys, and shiny shell-like pinks, and dark purples. The wall of the vagina was like a dark cave, purple-grey ridges reminiscent of a cathedral cut in stone, shadowy and even somehow threatening. And the cervix itself, pale pink and wet and shining: it was terribly poetic. Everything was magnified, so that the cervix virtually filled the enormous glowing screen. It was monstrous, a sci-fi nightmare, but at the same time the cervix was sort of breathtaking, if a bit lopsided and irregular, one of the effects of the DES.

I remember being amazed that all the people in the room were talking about my vagina while looking at the TV screen. I mean, I was used to them peering into me, and discussing what they saw, but now people could actually point at the TV screen, completely separate from me. They'd say, 'what about that bit?' in a kind of speculative tone, touching the TV screen with a finger, and then a gigantic wooden stick with a little wad of cotton wool on the end would suddenly appear, and sort of poke or prod the bit of my vagina or cervix pointed to, to see how it would respond. It seemed an extraordinary combination of extremely primitive behaviour (like a kid poking rotten leaves or mud with a stick he's found) with a kind of ultimate scientific hi-tech: the video image, in living colour, of my interior. I saw them apply the vinegar, and then the iodine, and I could even begin to make out what all the fuss was about, how the oddball cells didn't 'take up' the iodine the way you'd imagine they would. I began to feel a bit sorry for my cervix, exposed to all these eyes, this seemingly somewhat unscientific prodding. The light they shine up there is very bright and hot, like a spotlight; my cervix was like a reluctant star, caught in its flagrant glare.

The doctors seemed to be enjoying themselves, talking and gesticulating, when finally, the great man, the man in control of the camera, Doc Savage, this man put his hand gently on my inner thigh, he looked up from my cunt, and he said, 'Let's do a biopsy! Why not?'

Someone said, 'I wouldn't watch this bit if I were you.' Still, it was hard not to look. They take this extraordinary instrument like tongs, or scissors really, more like very long, thin scissors, with a little scoop on the end, and they cut a little piece of flesh out of your cervix. I saw the lump of red stuff on the end of the scissors when he pulled it out. Then they seal the wound they've made with silver nitrate; it reminded me somehow of the sulphur melting on the head of a match. I watched that bit. There's some bleeding. And then the doctors trooped out, and I was told to get dressed. It would take two weeks for the results of the biopsy to come through.

So I waited. Eventually I telephoned on the day I was told I could, and the head nurse said, 'We are writing to you.' And I knew that it must be O.K., otherwise they wouldn't write. So it was all over, until next time. And I was very happy, though quite exhausted emotionally by it all.

Then I called the nice Italian fertility doctor, and made an appointment with her. I thought, I'm going to get all this over with at once. I made the appointment, and I went to see her, I was practising my speech, my explanation, my request, and when I got into her office, out it all came. She told me I could have what's called an HSG, which is where they take an X-ray photo of your Fallopian tubes, to see if they're blocked or not. She said it would be interesting to see if the tubes had been affected by the DES, as well. I'd never thought of that.

When the day came I was very frightened, because I knew it was going to be painful, but also I was scared about what I would find out. As I was leaving I said to Patrick, 'This is what you might call elective torture.' I couldn't remember why I'd ever wanted to do this thing, but he reminded me, he said, 'You decided that if you had to have a terrible trauma about infertility, you might as well have it now.' It sort of made sense, vaguely.

I went to the hospital, and found the X-ray department with some difficulty. It was quite hilarious on one level, because everyone in the room – an enormous room, full of massive pieces of equipment – everyone was wearing lead aprons. I thought, where's *my* lead apron? As I lay down under this gigantic X-ray apparatus, I joked with the nurse, I said, 'I guess you don't have to work out at the gym if you wear one of those all day.' At first she didn't know what I was talking about, then she laughed. They were all pretty skinny.

The X-ray doctor was a young man, and he said, 'Why are we doing this?' I was slightly taken aback. I explained. Then I asked him what HSG stands for. He said, 'Hysterosalpingogram.' Then I said, 'This is like putting in an IUD, right?' and he said, 'Yes exactly, that's exactly what it's like.' Then he described the procedure. You lie down on an enormous table, with this massive machine hanging from the very high ceiling looming over you, very Frankenstein, and the doctor puts a speculum up you, and then he dilates the cervix (ow!) and inserts a catheter into it, and then he lines up the X-ray apparatus and squirts iodine (which is resistant to X-rays) into the uterus. The iodine fills the uterus, and then it runs down the Fallopian tubes, and spills out the ends where they form these sort of trumpet-like cones to catch the egg as it bursts out of the ovary. That's if they're unblocked. Otherwise, the iodine fills the tube to the point of scarring or blockage, and you can see where that point is. It's relatively straightforward. Then he takes the picture.

What was stunning, though, was the fact that again there was a little video monitor beside the examination table. The doctor uses the video image to line up the X-ray still camera, in order to get the best possible shot. He asked me if I wanted to watch, and I said, 'Of course.' This time the video image was like something out of 1940s science fiction, Buck Rogers maybe: it was black and white, and the image itself was oval, a kind of horizontal ellipse, framed within the black rectangle of the TV screen. And since of course X-rays aren't good for you (cf. lead aprons everywhere), the doctor would so to speak throw the X-ray on, in a kind of blast of light, and this very degraded, fuzzy black and white oval image of my pelvis would appear, momentarily, on the little TV screen, and then fade again, like a light going out. Again, it was terribly poetic.

I was tremendously uncomfortable, because I had all this equipment crammed in my vagina, and instead of being allowed to have my legs drawn up, like a frog, I had to lie them down flat, which was very difficult and very uncomfortable. I mean, it was painful, but you call it discomfort in that context, in the context of elective torture. So I had all this gear inside of me, this syringe of iodine and catheter and speculum, and my legs stretched out straight, and the doctor dressed in lead, adjusting everything with the help of brief bursts of X-ray video imaging. I could see the thigh bones fitting into the pelvis, and the metal instruments in my vagina. When he had everything lined up in the right position, he shot the iodine into my uterus. We both watched the oval

TV image. It was extraordinary: the little triangular uterus took form as the iodine filled it – the iodine appearing as flat white on this fuzzy TV screen – and then suddenly, momentarily, these two very fine lines were drawn, emerging from the points of the triangle, very fine lines meandering wildly like an ancient river delta. I'd always imagined the Fallopian tubes were like a sort of straight line, a tube from the ovary to the uterus, but they're not; they're very long, and very thin, and the iodine outlined their multiple curving zigzags until it reached the point where it spilled, a blurry fountain, out of the ends.

That meant the tubes were O.K. I was elated. The two fine meandering lines were drawn so quickly, instantaneously, it was like magic, and I watched it all, elated, in such painful discomfort and yet so elated, and at the same time thinking, how unbearable this would be if the tubes were blocked, and you saw it all, live on TV. It was like a shadow, the possibility of what it might have been like. As it was, I felt fantastic. The doctor took a couple of still X-rays of the configuration of uterus and tubes, and then slowly removed the instruments from my vagina.

I felt the opposite of what I've felt all these years, damaged; I felt like my dear old tubes had been under attack from all these drugs and diseases, and they'd survived somehow, they'd fended off the invasion, preserved themselves against the minuscule hordes of microbes and bacteria and poison. I always love that bit in *Notorious* when she says, 'They're poisoning me.' And there was something so perverse about figuring myself as feminine – as maternal, potentially – through the mediation of this elaborate medical technology, this technical imagining. A strange kind of reparation, some kind of return to the mother's body, via the fascinations of the video screen.

I'd pictured my mother's body, surging with artificial hormones, prescribed to her by idiots; my beloved mother who says to me, 'I took it very single day, from the third day of pregnancy to the moment you were born!' I'd pictured my own body: blocked, scarred, damaged. Now there was another image, almost unbelievable, narrow rivers meandering through the delta of my belly. The ghastly joke, the absurd literalization of the feminine metaphor that was my body, moved over, it shifted somehow. I didn't have to obsess about it any more, about the baby I wouldn't have; I could forget about it, now.

dilation

To Gina, the word daughter always sounded like it contained the word ought, the sound you make when gagging or retching. As a child, there were a number of different foods, like tapioca pudding, for example, which caused Gina to gag, or retch. Much later some of her worst nightmares contained an overwhelming, amorphous white mass, or shape, like a endless heap of shaving cream but more substantial, gelatinous, both fluid and solid, an image of absolute viscosity. She wondered if this were the tapioca pudding, come back to haunt her. Or perhaps, more ominously, her mother's gigantic white breast, an indelible memory of those first few weeks, of gagging, swallowing, and retching.

When Gina read that newborn babies always lose weight in the first ten days after birth, that the struggle with the mother for food invariably entails a certain element of difficulty, not to say starvation, she was profoundly comforted. So Freud was right, after all, she thought, there's no such thing as the perfect mother.

When Gina was fifteen, virginal, her mother said to her, in her mother's bedroom she suddenly turned to her, she spoke with vehemence, she said, 'You girls are so romantic about sex. Losing your virginity is awful, you really shouldn't have high expectations, it's hell. It hurts like hell, there's blood everywhere, you wake up in the morning all sticky, your legs all covered with –' At this point her mother hesitated momentarily, a conceptual hiccup in her tirade '– with the shoot-out from his penis,' she continued. 'It's *awful*.'

Gina thought, I think I'd rather maintain my romantic illusions than replace them with this insistent image of physical disgustingness. She tried to think of sticky thighs with some kind of enthusiasm. It was hard to imagine liking it.

Somehow, at this time, in her imagination, the sexual exchange of bodily fluids seemed bearable if they stayed in the appropriate place. The semen was meant to be in the vagina, not all over your legs. She couldn't do anything with it, this image too vivid and shocking to forget or efface.

Later Gina thought, why couldn't she just say 'come'. You wake up in the morning covered in come. Still, then, she probably would have found that an equally revolting idea, or word.

Later still Gina wondered at her mother's representation of sex. For years she'd interpreted pronouncements such as these to mean her mother didn't like it. Then she thought that was probably all wrong. (It was amazing how many people believed their parents didn't like it. As if the idea of them liking it were more than they could bear.) But her mother wanted to warn them, to protect her daughters, in case *they* didn't like it. Like it really wasn't very nice, and they ought to know.

*

When Gina was sixteen and three quarters, her mother and her older sister Amy were sitting in the kitchen, talking about losing your virginity. It was a hot topic in those days. Gina was standing at the sink, she was making coffee; her mother and sister carried on talking as if she wasn't there. They were talking about what the best age was, the best age to lose your virginity. Amy'd first done it at fifteen; that seemed a bit young. Finally they agreed sixteen was best.

Standing there, Gina smiled awkwardly, terribly shy, and said, 'I guess I haven't got much time.'

They both turned surprised faces up to her, and almost simultaneously, her mother and older sister cried, 'Oh *you'll* never lose *your* virginity, Gina!' Whereupon all three women fell about laughing.

When Gina was eleven she was sitting in the living room while her mother and a wonderfully glamorous girlfriend of her mother's drank coffee and smoked cigarettes and talked. She was very struck by a joke her mother's friend told, because she didn't understand it.

Three women are in the front seat of a convertible, driving down to a party in the country. One of them puts her hand out, in front of her face, and she says, I have such small hands, it's difficult to find gloves small enough and fine enough to fit them, they are so lovely and small. The second lifts up one of her feet and contemplates it, saying, I have the tiniest feet of anyone I know, they are so little and perfect. They go on and on like this for a while, showing off their tiny hands and little feet, until the third woman gets annoyed. Finally she says, has anyone got a band-aid? I think I've got the curse.

There was another joke, from that time, that Gina found equally perplexing. This one she read in a letter from her best friend, Zoë, who was out of town during the summer.

Why did Cinderella scream in the night?
Because her tampax turned into a pumpkin.

Another time, Gina heard her mother say, again to this very sophisticated, glamorous friend, she said, 'When my daughters are fifteen I'll just take them straight to the gynaecologist and have them fitted with IUDs. I mean, what else is one supposed to do?' It was 1967.

In the event, as her daughters got older, Gina's mother offered no contraceptive advice whatever. This was consonant with her previous practice in sex education.

When Gina was six, and her sister eight, her mother sat them down one summer afternoon, while Daddy was taking a nap. She said, 'I suppose you know by now how a man makes love to a woman?'

Both girls nodded solemnly. Amy said, '*You* don't know.' Gina said, 'Yes I do, you told me.' Amy said, 'No I didn't.' 'Yes you did,' Gina said. 'I never told you,' Amy said. 'You don't know anything.' 'Yes you did,' Gina said.

Only a few weeks before, Amy had forced this information on Gina, who felt no curiosity about it, if anything, a certain resistance to it. She knew she wouldn't like it, whatever it was.

Amy said, 'Do you know how babies are made?' Gina said, 'They come out of your stomach.'

Gina always imagined hospital doctors in white masks cutting you open, a huge gash across your tummy, to let the baby out. She was very anxious thinking about cavemen, though, because she knew they didn't have sharp knives then, or hospitals, or anything. She thought all the women in those times must have died when they had a baby, their stomachs bursting when the baby got too big. Then she thought, that can't be right. She thought they must have used sharpened flints, and sewed up the wound with sinew. It seemed both terrifyingly dangerous and somewhat unlikely. But how else could you get the baby *out*?

In any case, this vision of reproductive violence may have been one reason she was reluctant to hear what Amy had to say.

It was a similar problem to the question of the radio top ten, a question that plagued her a couple of years later. She didn't know how they decided a particular record would be number one. She came to the conclusion that all radios were secretly two-way radios, and the people from the radio station listened in, to hear what people were saying about the different records. She started talking to her clock-radio, mimicking realistic conversations, in which two or more voices discussed the Dave Clark Five versus the Zombies, in an attempt to get her favourite record into the top ten. After a couple of days of this, she gave up. It seemed too unlikely, simply. In Gina's world, apparently, there was no one she could ask about these things.

Amy said, 'No I mean how babies are made. What you have to *do*.'

Gina didn't know. She didn't want to know. She thought you got married and then the babies came along. She said nothing. Amy tormented her: 'Don't you want to know? Don't you want me to tell you?'

Finally Amy said, 'The man spits in your po-po.' (Po-po was the term the family used for vagina.)

Gina tried to pretend she wasn't shocked.

Gina's mother interrupted the two girls squabbling over who knew what. She may have been relieved that they were so certain she had nothing to tell them. She said, 'Well.'

They looked up. 'Well,' she said again, 'no doubt you think it's disgusting –'

At this the two children solemnly nodded again.

'But,' her mother said with a smile, 'we think it's *funny*!'

Funny? It was unimaginable. That was it, that was all the sex education Gina got from either of her parents.

When she was nine, one afternoon, Gina went downstairs to her mother's room and complained of a stomach ache. She didn't really have a very bad stomach ache, but she thought she might be able to extract some sympathetic attention, and maybe even stay home from school the next day. Gina put her hand flat on her belly, below her navel, and standing in the doorway of her mother's enormous bedroom, whining slightly, she said, 'Mummy, I have a stomach ache.'

Her mother seemed badtempered, more than a little annoyed. She asked Gina what she'd eaten, how long she'd felt badly. Then her mother snapped, 'Oh God, maybe you're getting the curse.' She sounded as if this would be the last irritating straw.

Gina didn't know what that was, the curse. She told her mother she didn't know what that was. Her mother flipped.

'You don't *know*?!' she shrieked quietly. 'How can you not know? Don't the girls at school talk about it?'

Gina said no.

'Don't you have any friends who talk about it?'

Gina started to feel frightened, her mother seemed so angry. Her mother said, 'Surely they teach you about it, don't they? Doesn't the school teach you about it?'

Gina said no, she didn't know what her mother was talking about.

Her mother went on, 'Don't the other girls talk about it? Don't the older girls talk about it, on the bus?'

Gina tried to reconstruct overheard conversations on the bus home from school. Maybe she'd misunderstood, her mother seemed convinced that everyone was talking about this, but she didn't know what it was. 'No,' she said.

Her mother heaved an enormous sigh. She looked slightly panicked as she realised she would have to explain.

'When girls get to be eleven or twelve or so,' she said, 'they get the curse. That means that every month they bleed a little instead of peeing. I mean, blood comes out, instead of pee.'

'Oh,' Gina said, in a deadened voice. She really didn't like the sound of that; she pictured a thin stream of bright red blood pouring out of her into the toilet.

'And sometimes you get cramps, in your stomach, too,' her mother said, raising her eyebrows hopefully.

Gina's stomach ache vanished like a shadow. She felt exhausted; she said, 'I think I'll just go lie down for a minute.' Her mother turned back to the mirror, turning back to the task in hand.

In the end, Gina figured it out by a process of deduction, logically. Her friend Sally said the man's penis went into you. This seemed horrifyingly plausible. But there must be, Gina thought, remembering the spit, there must be something else. The man must leave something there, inside you, something from his body. Sally denied this, she was certain he just put it in and that was it, the mere act of penetration was enough, but Gina was convinced. After much thought, she decided the man must pee a little, inside of you. That was how babies were made.

A couple of years later Gina's friend Zoë loaned her a book her parents had given her. It was called *Everything a Young*

Girl Should Know about Sex. It didn't say anything about contraceptives, or sticky come on your legs in the morning, but it clarified some things a bit. Nevertheless, when Zoë suggested that perhaps you would have to spread your legs, doing it, so that the man could get at that bit of you, Gina wasn't sure. It was hard to imagine, doing it.

Then they read Edna O'Brien's novel *The Country Girls*, in which at one point the heroine describes fucking her husband, lying flat underneath him, with the soles of her feet gently rubbing the small of his back. Gina spent a long time trying to imagine the position they were in, for this conjunction of sole of foot and lower back to take place. Eventually she got the picture. Thus Zoë's hypothesis was confirmed; you did open your legs.

When Gina was twelve she got her period. She was on holiday in Sicily with her family, sharing a hotel room with her sister. (Later she thought it was probably very D.H. Lawrence to have her menarche in Taormina.) Gina was terrified her mother would find out, and flip. She knew she would turn it into the most amazing drama. Gina tried to keep her bleeding secret from everyone, thinking, if I can just manage till I get back to London, only a couple of days, then I can go to the chemist and buy some pads. She changed her underpants many times a day, as each new pair became soaked with blood. In the evening, she scrubbed her underpants in the bathroom sink, with the door locked, carefully arranging them as she hung them to dry on the towel rail so that the blood-stained part wouldn't show. Her sister Amy figured out what was happening almost immediately, but said nothing. Later Gina wondered at Amy's discretion; was it embarrassment, or the sheer intensity of Gina's denial? Perhaps Amy dreaded her mother's reaction as much as Gina did.

The night before they were leaving for London, Gina's mother was in the girl's bedroom, supervising the packing. Gina sensed how lucky she'd been, that she'd managed to keep the secret so far. As Gina leaned over a suitcase on the floor, suddenly her mother emitted a yelp of anguish; she'd spotted some blood on Gina's pyjamas. 'Oh my God,' she cried, 'you've got the curse!'

There ensued precisely the grand opera Gina feared, with shouting and uproar, puffing sighs of irritation, screeds of words aimed in any direction, at Gina's sister, her father, at Gina herself. When Amy wearily acknowledged the situation saying, 'I know, I know, it's been going on for a few days,' Gina realised for the first time that pathetically draping her bloodstained pants around the bathroom in elaborately deceptive folds hadn't succeeded in concealing anything. When her mother gave her half a box of kleenex to put in her underpants, Gina wanted to disappear.

a question of lay analysis

Gina was having dinner at home with her friend Patrick. They sat together at the table, drinking red wine and eating fruit.

'What was so comic about the photography angle, though,' she said, 'was that I could see it too. I'd sort of got used to being the object of scrutiny, the archetypal passive position, right? And then technology intervenes, and suddenly I could look — at myself. I could line up with the experts, at the same time as being laid out for them.'

'For their delectation,' Patrick gently insisted.

'Quite. But the structure is shifted, somehow, isn't it? When the cervix becomes *my* cervix, and I can see it too.'

'What I keep wondering is,' Patrick said, 'if there's never anything wrong with you, isn't there something rather exhibitionistic about all this?'

'Exhibitionistic? *Moi?!*' They laughed.

'I know what you mean,' Gina said. 'This perpetual display, compulsively going down to the hospital to spread my legs, so to speak. To show something off, something that until recently I myself had never seen, some invisible symptom . . .'

'Yes,' Patrick said.

'So according to you, I'm really the active one, clambering onto the examination table and inviting the speculum in? How vile.'

'Well, I think it may be a bit of both,' Patrick said, prudently.

'What, active and passive. Maybe. I tend to think there are two possible bodies here, the body that's damaged but not dying, and the body that's really irrevocably fucked up. The test tells me which one is mine; it repeatedly reconfirms what I already know, the conditions under which I live: that something's wrong, but it's all right, for the time being.'

Gina paused, peeling her peach with wet fingers. Then she went on. 'The way I see it, it's a triangulation situation, in which the relationship of mother and daughter is mediated by this discourse of authority, medicine. I think the doctors must stand in for Daddy in some weird way.'

'But isn't it also all tied with stuff about damaging the mother's body, à la Melanie Klein?' Patrick asked. 'I mean, doesn't Klein say the classic crisis for the daughter is that she's already torn the mother's body to pieces, biting, scratching, gouging, gnawing — you name it.'

'I always envisaged a sort of explosion,' Gina said, 'the baby really wanting to just blow the mother's body up.'

'Mmm.' Patrick paused momentarily. 'So how come you're

so insistent that it was your mother who damaged you. I know Klein says little girls fear their mothers will –'

'*Eviscerate* them!' Gina shrieked.

'Precisely. So that turning the tables, reversing the terms, is part of a strategy of denial, maybe.'

'You mean,' Gina said, 'that I'm saying, again, I'm still saying, constantly, I'm saying: it's O.K., I'm already damaged, and my mother is the one who did this to me, and I can bear it. Really, it's O.K.'

'Yes,' Patrick said.

'So my accusation against her (*how could you do this to me?*) is actually a cover for my far more explosive and violent feelings, my fear of blowing her up.'

'Or a rationalization,' Patrick said. 'It's like, you won't submit to all that violence and passion, mother and daughter, daughter and mother. So you bring in a third term, you bring in the doctor and his, shall we say, *equipment*. You come up with another version – a version that's tolerable, barely, in which you're the one who's damaged, and you can cope, you can contain it, because she's the one who is in the wrong.'

Looking up, Gina spoke quickly. 'But what's so interesting is that in real life my actual mother doesn't seem to feel too bad about any of this stuff. She's terribly sane about it. First, she knows, she says, that there's nothing she can do about it. And then, she was only following doctor's orders, anyway; she was being the good little girl, or the good mother, gone awry. It's not her fault, in other words.'

'That clinches it, doesn't it?' Patrick said, smiling. 'Maybe if she'd responded differently to all this, if she'd shrieked and screamed, loud protestations of guilt and responsibility, maybe then you wouldn't have been able to use it as you have.'

'Which is?'

'Which is to be able to formulate an accusation against your mother, to accuse her of damaging you, irrevocably, without the fear of hurting her. She's well defended, she knows she was only trying to do the right thing.'

'I suspect she still thinks that if she hadn't taken all these precautions, she would have miscarried, and I wouldn't be here to complain about it. She didn't only take the drug, you know, she also spent a large part of the pregnancy in bed. Amy was two, or something, nearly two, and she just sat in the playpen watching TV, for months.'

'*Really?*' Patrick said.

'But recently when I thought I was pregnant, you remember, a couple of months ago, I talked to my mother on the phone, and she was telling me not to have too violent sex for a while, in case of causing a miscarriage, and I said, oh I have this theory of miscarriages, which is to let nature take its course, you know, maybe there's something wrong with the foetus, or whatever, and she roared with laughter and said, well if I'd thought that, you wouldn't be here now to have these theories!'

'So from her point of view, it really doesn't seem to be about her damaging you.'

'Absolutely not,' Gina said. 'From her point of view, it's another sign of love. But I have to hang on to this story, this tale of woe. I give her the power to harm me — in fantasy, I mean. If I imagine that she hurt me, then I don't have to deal with how much I might want to hurt her.' Gina paused.

'Or how much I *have* hurt her,' she said.

'Here we go!' Patrick exclaimed. Gina threw up her hands in mock despair, laughing, as Patrick got up to clear the table. He went into the little kitchen to make the coffee.

When he returned to the table, Gina was reading a book.

'There was this strange moment I never told you about,' Gina continued, putting the book to one side. 'That same time when I thought I was pregnant, and then my period came, violently, and I was so totally convinced I was having a miscarriage. You remember.'

'How could I forget?'

'Don't be mean. Anyway there was none of this let nature take its course routine, I was devastated, and filled with dread, you know, to have to go through it all again, and maybe miscarrying *again*, and suddenly, for one brief shining moment, in my desperation, I thought, if a doctor said, take this, and you won't miscarry . . . I would. For one moment, I occupied my mother's position, exactly, and I think that was when I forgave her, finally.'

A little later they were lying on the sofa, in each other's arms. 'I keep thinking about Harriet,' Gina said. 'I miss her.'

'Yes,' he said.

'But I keep thinking about how throughout her pregnancy she was completely obsessed with episiotomy.'

Patrick sat up. 'I've forgotten what that is,' he said.

'You know, where they make this neat cut, with scissors, at the bottom of the vagina, so it doesn't tear when the baby comes out. I mean, she was obsessed with tearing, the possibility of tearing, of being cut, and the question of being sewn up, and who would sew her up, and how. Like who was good at it, who was better, the midwife or the doctor, or what.'

'I guess it must be a bit like plastic surgery, irreversible. Someone sews up your vagina and maybe it's different to how it was before, and it *stays* like that.'

'That's right. *Horrible*. Though there's always stories of

women lying there after giving birth, saying, make it nice and tight, doctor!'

'Wow.'

'Anyway Harriet was obsessed with this, and then I was talking to Stella on the phone yesterday, I was telling her about Harriet, and tearing, and Stella said, *absolutely*. That's one of the reasons, she said, that she never wanted to have a baby. As if the baby being born caused such unimaginable damage to the mother's body, she couldn't even bear to think about it.'

Patrick said nothing. Gina went on, 'Stella said Harriet must have really wanted the baby, to overcome her fears of having her vagina torn to pieces.'

'So it's the mother again,' Patrick said.

'I think it's about a certain kind of narcissism, a sense of identity almost, a kind of narcissistic fixation, that's based on this image of a vagina. You know, a perfect vagina, or maybe just, *my lovely vagina*. And I think how weird that is, because I've never thought, my lovely vagina. I don't think I've *ever* thought that. I've always thought, my no good, damaged, odd, deformed, lacerated, weirdo vagina – that somehow has to manage, to make do. Because it's already damaged, in fact it's kind of a *mess* down there, and that's that.'

'So the lovely vagina, the perfect vagina is –'

'To me it's unimaginable, simply,' Gina interrupted. 'I can't really imagine how they would feel, Harriet, and Stella. Intact, maybe. Or something. I don't know.'

narcissistic disturbance

Above the desk, on the wall, there were two pictures. In one, Cézanne had painted a conch shell in such a way that it reminded Gina of a vagina. In the other, Georgia O'Keeffe had painted a cow's skull, with calico roses, in such a way that it reminded Gina of a vagina, a cunt.

Looking at one, then the other, hard and dry, sharp, the broken edges of the desert skull met the hard and shiny, cool contorted surface of the elaborate shell. The skull was white, the shell pink and red inside. A process of displacement, or metonymy, cunt to shell to skull, took place.

But cunts are wet and warm, not like this at all. The shell, the skull were (if they were) representations of vaginas that couldn't be fucked. As if they had the right qualities: elaborate interiors, a slit marking the opening where the inside and outside meet, the beautiful clitoris, undeniably there if you look for it, and that sense of further reaches, mysterious depths – this is the beginning place, the place of entry – but, not. The penis cannot penetrate this opening, it's too hard, too sharp. And the eye (blissful eye) can go no further, because a) it's a painting, flat, and b) you would have to cut, or break the shell, the skull, to pursue this knowledge, to see the inner recesses of the object.

The shell was particularly beautiful because of the colours, and the curling forms which were like a baroque fantasy of a cunt. The skull was particularly satisfying because the structure of the head, the horns, recalled the triangular structure of uterus and ovaries. It was anatomically congruent, yet pushed as far from direct reference as it could be. Gina wondered if Georgia O'Keeffe thought of it as a cunt, a clitoris, and then she thought it didn't matter anyway, and anyway she probably did, of course she did. It goes without saying.

The shell was part of a still life that included some things that reminded her of penises, a row of erect penises in the folds in the linen, a flaccid penis in the glass vase. There was also a black clock without hands. It was impossible to imagine that Cézanne was thinking, consciously, when he made this painting.

Looking at one, then the other, *the unfuckable vagina*, Gina thought. Too hard, too shiny. The phallus, more or less.

cleavage

The other day I passed a porno movie theatre on Hollywood Boulevard; it was showing a double feature: *Faces of Death/ Make Believe Is Not Enough*.

Let's face it, the body is always dying, on the verge of death – it's an embarrassment. The body is always embarrassing, and embarrassment is itself abject. The raw, the cooked, and the rotten – are we the rotten? Corrupt, diseased, deathly – fervently pursuing health or beauty while our cells rebel, metastasize, blossom into deathly flowers, or simply get tired.

Here in Los Angeles, the blank sun falls through poisoned air – air that destroys perspective, specificity of line and distance, in its unreal mist – this flat light falls on ideal bodies, hairless, muscular, on naked legs, bulky trainers and thick cotton socks, short denim skirts, bare midriff à la Madonna, endlessly permed hair. Every square centimetre of the body is tended, plucked, waxed, polished, inspected and adjusted. Exercise and liposuction and plastic surgery together keep it all in line, provide definition. Artifice is explicit in the heavy makeup (foundation, blusher, powder, lipstick, eye liner, lip liner, eye shadow, mascara) the women wear, despite the heat. Artifice is evident in the hair dyes, the perms, the cuts. Repeated exercises, supervised by personal trainers, reproduce identical muscles, ideal forms: the necessary dent in the upper arm, the sheer outline of a calf, a perfect thigh. Every body (almost) looks like this, each woman displaying the labour she has performed to make her body acceptable, ordinary. In this context, my pale, hairy legs are not merely an eccentricity, they're an abomination.

The other night I had dinner with a man who said he'd gone to a party in Beverly Hills with a bunch of very wealthy men and very pretty girls, and he'd thought, I don't want to tell these people I'm a writer, they couldn't care less about writers, in Hollywood writers are a dime a dozen. So he said he was a plastic surgeon. He said the women simply flocked to his side, he said they abandoned the promise of money for the promise of beauty, without hesitation. He said he was given what he called personal cards by six or seven beautiful women. He said that two of them, separately, had taken him upstairs, to show him their breasts. They both wanted to know: should they have had more?

I said, and what did you say? He said, I told them I thought they were fine.

Then he wrote an article about it. He talked to lots of women about why they'd done it, had silicone implants, and all of them said exactly the same thing: *so I could have a cleavage in a bathing suit.*

He said the problem with dating in L.A. is that as soon as you feel the silicone, it's not only unpleasant, unsexy, that is, but the woman also sort of falls in your esteem. What he said was, one thinks less of her, when one realises.

I said, you can tell? He said, you can tell immediately.

He said, he couldn't help it, he thought less of the woman, invariably, because he thought, she must be so insecure, to do that to her body. I said, well I can sort of understand cutting bits off – actually I can't, but I find it even harder to think of inserting bits of plastic *into* your body. He agreed. I told him that the last time I was in London, my older sister said, I'll never have plastic surgery, never, never, never, let's make a pact, we'll never have plastic surgery. And I'd said, sorry, I can't promise I won't! He nodded seriously, sympathetically, and said, well, yes, now you live in L.A.

Another man I know told me, lovingly and amazed, almost reverentially, he told me that in labour his wife turned into an animal. Is that it? Is it birth, sex, food, shit that makes the body abject? What could be more abject than these breasts that continue to stand up even when you're lying flat on your back? They only work, they only look good when you're standing up, the man at dinner the other night told me. When you lie down, the fact that they don't sag is terribly disconcerting. Uncanny.

Or is it that all those things, food and shit and sex, are merely stand-ins for death — death which is always with us, just under the surface of the skin. All you have to do is make an incision, open a little door, and death springs out, red as blood, and grabs you by the throat. He's always there — like my grandmother used to say about men, she'd say, men are like streetcars, there's always another one just around the corner. That's where death is, just on his way, just around the corner.

such pleasures

Gina went round for a drink with Beatrix, who told her this story:

'It was said that what he really liked was fucking dead women. So the women who went out with him played dead.

'It would take some time to persuade them, one imagines, to talk them into it, but it was said that some of these women, the girlfriends, the lovely blondes, would submit to his will, or his wish. They would agree to be knocked out, in order to afford him these pleasures. They were all on drugs half the time anyway, so maybe it wasn't such an extreme request, to suffer an injection and go under for an hour or two. Unconscious.

'He would administer the drug by injection, and then he would fuck her. And, it was said, that once the woman was out, unconscious, he would place her body in a freezer for a while – I imagine an enormous horizontal freezer in the larder or scullery next to the kitchen in his Mayfair flat, its coffin-like lid left open, her head sticking out, hanging over one end, as thin icy fog rises in wisps around her pale flesh.

'He would place her body in the freezer for a while, so that it would be cold when he fucked it. More lifeless, less lifelike. Less like a coma, more like dead.'

What Gina couldn't understand or imagine was how anyone could take pleasure in not knowing what was happening to them or what he was doing to them. It seemed an act of trust beyond her wildest dreams. 'How would you know you would ever wake up again?' she said. 'When he approached you with the hypodermic – no, this is taking masochism too far, this is beyond fantasy, much closer to an elaborate form of suicide, no?'

Beatrix was more comprehending. 'On the other hand,' she said, 'you have to admit, there's a tremendous power in giving pleasure up, in renunciation.'

She went on, 'And then supposedly he would be grateful, or something, for letting him do it to you, and he'd want to do it again. He'd stick around. It's called how to keep your man.'

LESLIE DICK

'The mechanism of poetry is the same as that of hysterical phantasies.'

Freud

TO FIND WORDS

Lynne Tillman

I have nothing to say. There is nothing to say is another way to say it. Or, still another way, there is so much to say, and so many ways, should I begin? May I begin? Do I need to ask your permission? I promise you delight. I promise you a real good time. I promise you the best. This will be the very best, the best you've ever had. I am a ride, a roller coaster, the fun house. I'm what frightens you in the palace of horror. I'm pleasure. I'm a drive in the backseat of a car late at night when the moon is full and everyone else is asleep. I'm sex. I'm compassion. I'm the tears on your cheek when you say goodbye forever to that handsome but pitiful character in the movie you love. Now I'm anger and outrage, fire engine red inside your brain. I'm choking you with rage. I'm the pain that dwells in your gut which you cannot express to anyone. I'm the ache in your heart. It hurts. You hurt. You cannot speak. Lie down, make yourself comfortable, adjust the light. I'll speak for you.

That's the problem. And I could go this way or that, tell this story or that. I could seem to believe in words, I could pretend to believe in words and in the power of stories. I could insist: I am a storyteller. I could take comfort in conventional wisdoms and make many references, shoring up my position, to defend myself to you and from you. I could hate words, distrust language, forego stories. I could do all this, everything. I could use everything, I could try it all.

I could, but I don't want to. I don't care, though that's not entirely true. It is partially true and partial truths are after all what one must settle for. If one settles. I don't know about you, but I feel like hell. The country is falling apart, what does anything matter, people are dying, starving, being blown out of the sky, people are suffering, and what does anything matter, what difference does this nothing make, what matter do words make?

When she awoke, she could not speak at all. I didn't let her swallow, she felt she could not breathe, her throat was dry, she drank many glasses of water, she went back to bed and fretted silently. Words danced in front of her, a ballet that no one would comprehend. This word partners that? She could not swallow, that damned, fucking, horrible lump in her throat. It is not the first time. It happens often. Such a weird sensation.

It's terrible that I am her voice because she depends on me. She is to be pitied. She looks sad, lying there in her mother's nightgown. Her mother is dead. Suddenly she sits up, puts a notebook on her lap, and finds a pen on the floor, the pen she threw away last night (oh last night). She writes in her notebook. Her other hand is wrapped lightly about her throat as if she were gagging herself.

'The Body has a Mind of its Own
The Mind Speaks through its Body
The Body Speaks its Mind
The Mind has a Body of its Own

'To write a story is to be in a state of hysteria. Writers call up from their minds and bodies (I do not make a separation) memories, ideas, fragments of thoughts, images. The fragmented story is symptomatic, and like a symptom of the hysteric, who cannot retrieve the whole, it is stymied by a regrettable and important loss from a particular scene that would make the story complete. But even the narrative that we think of as well-formed, the traditional narrative, with a beginning, middle and end, that too is of necessity a fragment, which the writer, to counter loss, is impelled to produce. All writing is hysterical. The body always speaks.'

This was the voice that Paige Turner initially chose, from many possible voices, I might add, to begin a story about hysteria. She had studied and studied, thought and thought, and from all that she had read, and from all that was in her, so to speak, Paige decided to sally forth with a jab at the problem of writing itself. It is one possible approach. Sally go round the roses.

It doesn't seem to me that it is exactly the right voice or precisely the right way to begin. The first line of a story is like the first impression one can never make again. You never get a second chance to make a first impression. I am not completely sure and neither is she. And it is this that I have reminded her: Is this your voice? Couldn't anyone else have written this? Who is speaking? And, of course, who cares?

Paige Turner is a tall woman, with bright red hair. She is a petite woman with jet black hair. She is of middling height, has blonde hair and is known to diet strenuously and laugh loudly. Today her cough is constant; she hates what she has written. She will not begin her story that way, but it will plague her. Paige worries that the ideas she thinks urgent won't be understood. On the other hand overstatement worries her more. She thinks this and glances at her other hand. There is dirt under two of her nails. Red polish peels off both thumbnails. Her hands look injured, as if they've been to war. She will apply more red polish to her short, dirty nails. One hand is shaking. This is beyond her control.

When Paige was just a child, she would shake at the kitchen table, shake her leg so vigorously that her father would joke: Will that be a chocolate or a vanilla milk shake? Paige shakes her head, to forget the moment and his expression, what he said as well as the look on his face. A look of bemusement, mockery or tenderness. The look that she remembers, the look she invents again and again, is a jumble in her mind which she thinks of as a kind of messy store where her trinkets and junk are displayed, where other people's souvenirs, other people's pasts, are represented, all as small objects. Precious memory. Her throats hurts. She swallows hard. She cannot speak.

I call her Little Miss Understood. Naming is everything. Sticks and stones will break your bones and names will always hurt you. Names will make you cry. A comic and ominous taunt to Little Miss Understood sitting at her Underwood. On days that are wet and grey or on bright blue ones, it drives her crazy. Mad, wack, nuts, bonkers, ape shit, and so on. I drive her out of her mind. She wants to do the driving herself. She walks back and forth mumbling aloud, speaking to herself. She tells herself that it is a mark of intelligence to talk to oneself — she read this in a popular psychology column written by Dr Joyce Brothers, for Vogue magazine. She takes comfort in such reassurances. She sits at her desk, pulls at her hair, jerks her leg and sorts through paper. She opens books and stares into space. She looks at old photographs of herself and her family, of lovers and friends. Sometimes she imagines she is staring inward, as when she pretends that the outside is the inside. Have you ever tried that? At other times she gazes at the pictures on her walls to invigorate her mind, to catch herself unaware, to startle herself with new meanings. There is a lump in her throat.

'I look for a hair that might have lodged between my lips when eating. It has been swallowed and sits in my throat, tickling me, tickling my fancy. I have eaten hair. Disgusting? Disgust is interesting. Voices can be disgusting. Insinuating, dirty. A voice from the past. I will tell the dirty old man story. Every woman has a dirty old man story.'

She is hoarse, her voice deep in her raw throat. But she begins to write, which I think takes pluck, shows stubbornness or demonstrates a kind of silliness, a deep silliness deep in her deep throat. I ought not trivialize the task before her, but how can I not? I remind her how foolish she is. She glances at the ceiling, distracted. She touches her throat and coughs. She calls to me, her disembodied voice. Be still, lie down, rise up, die, live.

'She was sick to her stomach. The bus ride was supposed to take five hours, but it was raining and the slick roads caused the driver to go slowly. Time was dragging, moving along with the labored swish of the window-wipers. Time was dumb and slow. She liked buses better than trains because the lights were always off in buses if you rode late enough at night. She was returning to college. She'd eaten so much during the weekend at home that she could barely move. She opened the button at the top of her pants. Her mother had made a chocolate cake which she'd finished when her family had gone to bed. She vomited in the morning but she knew she'd gained weight anyway.

'The man next to her stirred. He'd been sleeping since the beginning of the trip. Now he was awake. He was old and his face was covered by stubble. He was fat too. He started to talk to her. He ran a fast-food chicken place on Second Avenue, he asked if she'd ever been there. She said no. She was glad to talk even though he was ugly. In the light he would be even uglier so she was glad it was dark in the bus. After a while she didn't know what else to talk about because she didn't think he'd be interested in what she was studying or the fact that one day she was going to be a writer. She was too selfconscious to say any of it anyway. It seemed stupid.

'So she closed her eyes. She covered herself with her coat and pretended to go to sleep. He didn't do anything for a while. Then he placed his hand on her pants, first on her thigh, and then he moved his hand there. He began to rub her. No one had ever done that. She didn't know what to do. She didn't think she wanted him to stop because the feeling was strange and nice. She knew it was wrong but it didn't matter that it was. She watched the feelings she was having. She felt very far away. Then she became more and more uncomfortable. She felt hotter. She pretended to wake up and went to the bathroom. There are always bathrooms on Greyhound buses. Everyone else was asleep. She was really alone. Inside the small toilet she felt her underpants. They were wet. She went back to her seat and told the dirty old man, "I know what you were doing and it was wrong. Don't do it again." The words came from outside of her, as if spoken by an intruder. It was a strange voice, almost unrecognizable.'

I disgust her. She returns to bed. She is discontented. The story may not be right, the voice off. Unsure, she shrinks from herself. She is too little to live. To love. She is too big. There is no time to be content. I disgust her. The hair tickles her throat, her fancy. Her fancy is a lump in her throat.

The saying, I have a lump in my throat, is used generally, in English anyway, when someone feels a great burst of sad emotion, a swelling of emotion. Emotion seems to swell and gets stuck in the body, odd though that may be. The swelling becomes physical, something is stuck in one's throat. Often I become a thing in her throat, as if she'd swallowed a great obstacle and it lodged there. I don't mean she actually swallowed an obstacle. I mean I am the lump in her throat, which is an obstacle. As she writes the dirty old man story, she loses her voice – a case of laryngitis. She cannot speak above a whisper. She wonders if her loss is also her gain, one voice for another. She wonders if she is a whispering woman. She coughs.

'A woman I know attended a private screening of a film. Jackie Kennedy Onassis entered the small cinema, with another woman. Jackie Onassis stood close to my friend who was sitting at the end of the row. She had never seen Jackie O. in person. It was peculiar because she felt she had grown up with her. Jackie O. had recently had a facelift and she looked much younger than she was. That was peculiar too. Jackie O. whispered loudly to her friend, who had red hair and was as tall as she. The whisper was a stage whisper. It could be heard all through the room. When the two sat down in front, Jackie O. kept whispering, her head inclined close to her friend's. But when the movie started, she stopped and sat absolutely still in her seat, not moving. Not once during the entire movie did she move. She was fixed in her seat. That too was strange. The movie ended and Jackie O. and her friend walked out behind my friend. Jackie O. was still whispering. Afterward there was a lavish reception. My friend took a seat on a couch and drank wine. She saw Jackie O. talking to some people. My friend thought, I'm glad not to be introduced to her. What could I possibly say to her? Later she mentioned this to her lover. He said, "You could have asked her if she saw anything on the grassy knoll." They laughed for a long time, imagining how Jackie O. might respond. They knew she wouldn't. I told my friend I'd once heard that Mary Todd Lincoln also whispered. But whether she whispered after Lincoln's assassination or whether she whispered all her life, I didn't know.

'The next day I read in the *New Yorker* magazine about a woman who had placed her mother in a nursing home. The woman's mother warned her, "If you do this to me, you'll never sleep again." The woman developed insomnia on the day her mother entered the home. She has not slept regularly since.'

Paige might call this 'The Whispering Women'. I remind her that the mother did not warn her daughter, You will lose your power of speech or stutter for the rest of your life. That would be germane. But Paige likes the insomnia story. It gives her goosebumps just to think of it. It makes her flesh crawl. It makes her look behind her to see if someone is standing there. She has a coughing fit. She is thinking and she is not thinking. She may be dreaming.

Paige's mother is in a nursing home. On the day she left her there, and after parting from the reluctant, tearful, elderly woman, Paige came down with the flu. It turned into strep throat. And she lost her voice. Who could she have talked to about it anyway, she thought.

To find words, to find words from all the possible words. It's a game, like stick the tail on the donkey or treasure hunt. The hunt may or may not offer a reward at its conclusion. The game cannot be Monopoly. You know that. To find words and place them in sentences in a certain order. Syntax.

'There is a sin tax in the U.S. on liquor and cigarettes, on luxuries, but what are luxuries. What isn't necessary and who decides that?'

If I let her find words she will rush to form sentences. She will rush to judgment and will try to make sense. Can she? She persists. Sense and nonsense. Words free, unfixed. Paige longs to make music with words, to discover the moment when words vibrated in the body. She wants to discover time inside herself, to give rhythm to her sentences. Style is rhythm. Rhythm is style. She hears a drumbeat, then a bass line, tough and funky. She imagines the inside is the outside. She is greedy for everything. She opens her mouth wide. If words could make wishes come true. If wishes were horses she'd ride away. Paige wants a voice like the wind.

I tell her: The wind has a voice but I cannot mimic it. The wind has its own music. The wind howls, everyone says so. It is a wolf. I cannot be a wolf. I cannot howl. When I give voice to a thought — do you like that? — it may sound scratchy. Her voice may sound thin, a scream vibrating at a frequency unbearable to dogs or wolves. Do you find that amusing? I had to urge those words from the vocal box into the mouth and onto the tongue. She repeats them. Her tongue is pink and whitish and scalloped at the edges. She is neither proud nor ashamed of her tongue. She can't touch her chin with her tongue. She rarely thinks of her tongue but when she does, she begins to imagine that her tongue is too large for her mouth. When she realizes this feeling, she gets small sores on the sides of her tongue. Then she remembers her mother telling her, when she was little, Don't get too big for your britches. Paige didn't know exactly what britches were, then.

'I dreamed that I was with a man who was a psychoanalyst. We were sitting in a circle, I was opposite him. There were other people in the circle too. He told me that he had been looking up my skirt. He spoke indifferently. I said to him indignantly, surprised, "I'm used to wearing pants, not skirts. I am very angry that you continued to look up my skirt and didn't warn me."'

Her sister takes her to a shopping mall which turns into a medieval castle. Paige doesn't remember this part of the dream. Anyway, if she publishes it, it's not her dream any more. She shakes her head, rubs her eyes, pours a cup of tea and has the sense – sensation settling in her throat, words are stuck there – that she's forgotten to telephone someone. Or that she's lost something of importance. She shakes her head again. A friend who does Yoga once insisted it was possible, with a vigorous shake of the head, to rid oneself of bad thoughts. Paige doesn't believe it but she does it anyway. She intones silently: Let it go, let it go, let it go.

She blows her nose. Crumpled up tissues, the day's detritus, are strewn about the room. In a drawer, the second drawer in her dresser, the dresser she inherited from her grandmother, there are handkerchiefs with *Paige* embroidered on them. She likes to blow her nose into linen handkerchiefs, especially those bearing her name. She runs to the dresser and does just that. She laughs out loud. She feels unwell.

Then she telephones a friend but there is no comfort, no release. Her friend says she can barely hear Paige, and why doesn't she see a doctor? They say goodbye. Paige's throat aches. She sits down at her desk.

Words plague her and push through her body, brazenly, hazardously, forced by the breath, the breath of life. Her lungs work furiously, her heart beats rapidly in a kind of rhythm, a pulse beat: I love you, I love you, I do. I'm thinking of you all the time. Can you hear my heart beat? It's a furious melody, it's a cacophony, this insistent incessant crazy love I have for you. You're always near. You never go away. Paige thinks she's going to scream. She might not be able to restrain herself. But can she scream? Does she have it in her? If she screams, the neighbors might think she was being murdered.

'A scream ripped from her, tearing the air, renting it as if it were silk. A scream – in the middle of the night, in the middle of a party. Everyone sat there, their hands shaped like cups and saucers. They were indifferent to her, preening. It was not unusual for people to watch themselves in mirrors and admire their images. Oddly enough those people who looked longest were considered the most beautiful. The scream, everyone said, meant nothing.

'She was not without charm. Silky hair fell in waves about her face, covering one of her clever eyes. She clasped her pale hands, crossed her long legs, held herself erect. She lowered her gaze, embarrassed and yet oddly proud. He danced toward her, embraced her and then regaled her with stories of places she had never been. After this she did a slight dance that went unobserved by everyone but the tea drinker. The tea drinker gestured, beckoning with compassion. She caught the look but acknowledged it a little too seriously. Both grew uncomfortable.

'In the corner, too close to her, was a man who repeated himself endlessly. He had a square jaw. She listened to him and could not listen to him. He spoke in a monotone but even so he was sometimes perceptive and entertaining, in a tragic sort of way. They had once been lovers for reasons she could not fully remember. And one day, suddenly, she no longer wanted him to penetrate her. The very thought of making love with him became abhorrent to her. He could not understand her reluctance to engage in an act they had done many times before. But then he repeated himself endlessly, so how should he understand?

'Her brothers strode into the room. The sight of them caused her a simultaneity of pain and pleasure. She was speechless. She wished they would leave. An old feeling, a dusty antique gown, wrapped her in perpetual childhood. She feared she must stay there always. She wanted to believe something else. The room enclosed her. She could not breathe. She was a fish out of water. She was an uninvited guest. A stranger, a madwoman, a whore. She was an explorer who didn't like what she found. She swooned. She screamed.

'The scream came from someone she did not know, as if a lodger had taken a room in her without her consent. The scream was unpleasant, though not completely unmusical. It was pitched high, at the top of a tall tree, at the top of a winter tree, bare of leaves, stark against a steel-grey sky. Naked branches, fingers pointing to the abyssal sky, would scream the way she did if they could.'

The words lie there and they may be lies. They lie on the page. They are little worms. Once she dreamed, on the night before a reading she was to give, that rather than words on paper, there were tiny objects linked one to another, which she had to decipher instantly and turn into words, sentences, a story, flawlessly, of course. Funny fear of the blank page. Didn't she recently explain that writing was erasure, because the words were already there, already in the world, that the page wasn't blank.

In the room there is no sound other than her own breathing and the rattle of the windows. An eerie sound. The wind is blowing hard against them. The windows may shatter. Their rattling is like a wheeze from a dying person. A death rattle, a wail. The buffeted windows emit a sad human sound. Paige is sensitive to sound, the way some people are sensitive to smell. Her mother was an opera singer, a soprano who quit midcareer to marry Paige's father. Sometimes her mother would sing when she did housework. When Paige was little she disliked her mother's voice. Later she admired it.

Paige doesn't like the sound of her own voice. When she has laryngitis, her voice settles deep in her throat and sounds raspy. Call it sexy. Do you think so? Perhaps the voice intimates a threatening possibility. It may be saying: I come from down here. I am in your body. I am, like you, from an animal. I growl. I am covered by soft hair. I go out of control, I like to be touched, and were you to reach inside me and find that hidden place, it would surprise you. It would terrify you. The urgency is raw and harsh, like this voice that has been taken away, taken by the wind or gods or ancestors. When I cannot talk at all, will you listen to me?

'It is the night of the world. Life is dark and hidden from me. The animals cannot sleep. The mountains are complacent and stalwart. The caves are shy, without light. The plains don't want to be flat. The desert is listless, waiting. I have been sitting here a very long time listening to the wind as it races past. It is howling and wailing, it is crying. It pules. It shakes the glass in the windowpanes. I stare out into the dark night. I am completely alone, my hand caresses my neck. The beauty of the world stretches away from me.'

Paige pats her left shoulder absentmindedly. She strokes her neck. She has a long thin neck upon which her head balances precariously, like an exotic bird's might, a salmon pink bird that can be found only in a hot southern clime. Paige has never been to the tropics. It is cold in the room. Her throat is sore. It hurts like a broken window.

'Where does the wind rush and why does it gallop away? How to describe the fascinating horror of natural forces, to describe the body of the world which envelops me and exists outside my body? The house is old. It is old enough to be an antique. The shadows in the room obscure the objects in it. I sit on a chair made of dark wood. I am wearing blue cotton pajamas that my father once wore. Blue is the color of hope. I nursed my father for many years before his death. He died of throat cancer. At the end he could not speak. I have my memories. They are fixed and still like his dead body. It is almost morning but the sun has not yet completely risen.'

The effect wasn't what she wanted. Paige probably ought to weave these paragraphs into the scream story. It might work. It might fit. It might be fitting but she cannot decide. She is lost at sea and cast in doubt. She is scrambling for words and glances helplessly at her books. Her guard is down. Right now, were you to criticize her or, worse, insult her, she'd be stunned, crushed. Look: She crumples before your sharp eyes, her face falls, actually falls, as if the bones that construct it and the skin that the bones support had given up, given her up, given up on her. Crestfallen, she is as helpless as an animal that has had the misfortune to be shot with a tranquillizer dart.

Have you ever seen an elephant go down when injected with such a drug? A sorry sight. The elephant drops like a sack of concrete; it falls like a building exploded by dynamite. One can watch it happen in nature films, which Paige likes very much. Animals move her in a way that human beings never do. She will not admit this nor will she write about it. Her parents gave away her dog. She didn't talk for weeks. Her calico cat ate her powder blue parakeet. The cat was given away. She was beyond words and didn't even write about it in her diary. Her father asked: Cat got your tongue, Paige?

'It is in the unconscious that fantasy, moments of the day, and memory live, a reservoir for the poetry of the world. Is everything else prose? Is what's conscious ordinary prose, the prose of the world?'

Or, I tease, the pose of the world. She is separating much too neatly the world she knows – I nearly wrote word for world – from the world she doesn't know, the one that owns her and to which she is a slave. She is a slave to what she can't remember and doesn't know and she is a slave to what she remembers and what she thinks she knows. Her education has damaged her in ways she does not even know.

Paige suffers mainly from reminiscences. Memories come in floods, in half-heard phrases, in blurry snapshots. They merge into one another. They have no edges. They emerge in the mountains, in movie theaters, in fields, on the road; they erupt in rooms, in cafés, when she walks, they come all the time. They come when she is talking to friends. They come and her friends disappear in front of her as she fights to clarify a faded image, reassemble a dubious moment, inhale a familiar scent.

Impossible past, what did that perfume smell like, what did his voice sound like, where does the air linger so sweetly, where did her train set go, where was the playground, who are the small people playing funny, frightening games, who called her name. What is whispering? She is captive to impossibility. She opens her notebook then turns on the radio. An advertisement asks: 'Would you like to speak French? It's easier than you think.' On the news a missile is referred to as a 'technological hero'. She turns off the radio. She chooses music from many cassettes which are piled one on top of the other. Her hand covers her mouth, an old gesture, and she coughs; then her index finger slides free and touches her top lip. She looks as if she is musing, being her own muse.

One of Paige's favorite songs, 'I'm Your Puppet,' was recorded by James and Bobby Purify. It was popular years ago, but she didn't know when it was written, and maybe the Purifys – purify, could that really have been their name? – maybe they were no longer alive. No matter when she heard the song, morning or night, and no matter where she was, she always felt what she felt when she heard the song for the first time. Paige can even remember where she was and with whom: near her high school, in a fast-food joint, with a rock and roll musician; and she even remembers what he said to her about the song – he was curious why she liked it so much, wasn't she perverse? She remembers how she felt when the tune ended and also when the relationship ended, curiously and insignificantly.

'Pull a string and I'll wink at you
I'm your puppet

I'll do funny things if you want me to
I'm your puppet
I'm yours to have and to hold
Darling, you've got full control
Of your puppet . . .'

Paige is dancing in front of the mirror. She is moving her hips. She is swaying, her eyes are closed, she is traveling, she is faraway. Sinuous motion. She is everywhere and nowhere.

'Just pull them little strings
And I'll sing you a song
Make me do right or make me do wrong
I'm your puppet.'

After she listened to it over and over, she wondered if the Purifys actually felt like puppets, and then she wondered why she cared. It was a song they sang. They didn't write it. Maybe they hated singing it. Maybe they didn't like the melody. Maybe they hated the words. Paige can give you the lyrics, not the tune. Do you know the song and do you hear it when you read the words?

Paige knew a woman, just a girl really, who had memorized practically every song that had ever been written, and she could play and sing beautifully. They met in Berlin, on a summer day, as the Wall came down. The girl had a guitar strapped to her back. Paige swallows hard and remembers Agnes. Agnes is a lump in her throat.

'Agnes was tall – oh Agnes, agony – so tall, she could have played pro basketball if she were a man, and she was built like one, bearing broad shoulders and a heavy jaw.

Instead she played the guitar in a militant way typical of those still influenced by Dylan and Odetta. She played when she begged on the street, near the subway at Astor Place, which is where I usually found her, standing not far from a woman in her fifties who did small paintings she sold for a dollar, usually religious themes in a wild style. I bought many, for a dollar, a bargain, and gave them to friends, and some knew they were worth something, that there was a special kind of mind at work in those small paintings, with their vivid blues and muted greens. She might use as background a lime yellow and dot some rose on it, the rose was a rose; or the theme was religious, something like nuns talking on telephones, as if in direct communication with god.

'Agnes ignored the painter. Agnes didn't like art, it didn't seem to her to serve the purpose music and words did, didn't speak to her, and she was deeply involved in speaking. Agnes talked all the time or sang all the time. She tended to shout the later at night it was, the closer it came to the time when she should have gone home if she had had a home, which she didn't. She stayed with me once, but only once, because she wanted to talk all night about music and writing. I wanted to watch *Hill Street Blues* or something soothing: the captain of the precinct and his wife the lawyer end up in bed, to love away their troubles or to discuss stoically their harrowing day, one filled with more catastrophe than anyone else's. Except maybe Agnes's. I like to be in bed when people on television are in bed. But not Agnes, she didn't want to sleep and could talk all night and I don't know when she slept. She could talk endlessly. I think she liked the sound of her own voice.

'Agnes was unattractive. Her lumbering awkwardness seemed to come from her difficulty in just being alive, of her being acutely aware of her bulky frame and plain face. She must have conceived of herself as a burden to behold. She walked with her head down. She stooped over, bending herself to the ground to make her big body less significant or impressive, less noticeable. Tall people stoop over which is why they often have bad backs. I read that in a book I proofed about back pain – I work as a proofreader – I'd never thought about back pain before and after I finished it, having read that it can happen at any time, out of the blue, that you can turn your head, or pick up a cup, and boom, your back goes out and you're in pain for weeks, there was something else to worry about, something else to be anxious about that could happen to you seemingly at random. But can anything that happens in your body be at random? I told Agnes to stand up straight but she wouldn't listen and I'm sure she'll be a stooped old woman if she lives that long. But where is Agnes? Did she go back home to Minnesota? Will I hear that voice of hers again?

'Agnes pretends not to suffer. That's her glory. She depresses me but then I'm not able to suffer happily the way she does. Agnes is the most Christian person I know. She doesn't hate anyone and carries her belongings around with her as if nomadism were her chosen lot in life, not simply a sign of her poverty. Most every day I'd see her and sometimes I'd take her for a coffee or a bowl of soup at a diner. She was remarkably presentable and never smelled. I have to admit that if she did I wouldn't have been able to go around with her. It's gotten so I can't walk into some restaurants because of the stench of cockroach spray. It suffocates me. I move away from people who have bad breath. What's happening in their bodies, I wonder. I don't know where Agnes bathed or showered but she kept herself clean. She had her secrets and lived in a secret way. I don't know what's happened to her though, she's not around, and it's so cold out. Will I ever hear her sing again? Her voice cut into the night like a knife.'

Cut to: interior – a studio apartment in Manhattan. It is raining. Paige is sleeping. She awakens and begins to cough. She has no voice. She remembers her dream. In it she is making love with a man. He wants her desperately, the passion is incredible, huge, overpowering, bigger than both of them. But he is impotent. They stop. They start again. He cannot. His flesh is weak. Then he crawls into her arms and lies across her lap. They form the Pietà. In the dream she says to him, So you would rather be the baby than the penis.

In another dream her father is alive. He speaks to her. Then he dies in front of her, as he always does in her dreams. She comforts her mother, in the dream, by saying, At least I was able to hear his voice again.

'Cut to: A woman at her desk, writing her dreams furiously. She is laughing, she is crying. She tears one sheet of paper out of the typewriter, then another, and another, and after several hours of intense work, she has a pile of papers in front of her. Victoriously she prints 'The End' at the bottom of the last page.'

How Paige wishes her life were scripted. How she wishes for inspiration, though she does not find it and doesn't believe in it. Must one believe? How she wishes she did. If wishes were horses . . .

> 'Pull another string and I'll kiss your lips
> Snap your fingers and I'll turn you some tricks
> I'm your puppet

Your every wish is my command
All you gotta do is wiggle your hand
I'm your puppet.'

If Paige continues and even finishes the Agnes story she might title it 'Ordinary Unhappiness'. Though maybe Agnes's was neurotic unhappiness. Maybe it ought to be called 'Dramatic Pictures'.

Dramatic Agnes wasn't easy to forget. She lingered in Paige's mind, in the air, as vaporous memory. You might say Agnes was unique. You might say she was pathetic. Wounded certainly, a wounded baby animal. Paige hears Agnes's clear voice as if she were singing in the room, beside her. Then inside her. Agnes's voice quivers in Paige, strikes a knowing chord, hits a funny bone.

Surely you know people like Agnes. Their voices are sheltered in your body. They have become phrases in your body. They are your visitors. Sometimes you push them away, push them out, exhale them heavily. You don't want them inside you. You may want to kill them. I don't want them either. I am too full and too empty. The bombs are falling. People are maimed, dead. I can barely think, let alone speak. What should I do? I must offer you something. I must prove something, I have something to prove. I will prove it to you. Words will be transformed into wishes.

Paige is holding her head in her hands. Noises from the street disturb her, urge her from her chair. She rushes to the open window. The neighbors, Debbie and Ricky, are fighting again. They are screaming, their faces ugly, their bodies twisted, distorted by fury and drugs.

'Back home, Jesus says to me, "Debbie likes to get hit, man, she's sick. Ricky tells her to stop yelling and then slaps her and she goes, More, more, hit me again." I don't know whether or not to believe Jesus. I don't want to. But I've never known him to lie. He asked me once, "Are you going to write about my family? It'd make a bestseller, it's a horror story. Everybody'd want to read it. They'd make a movie about it. You'd make millions."

'Jesus plays basketball with the guys who hang out across the street. Some come from other neighborhoods. Jesus is the only one of his family who's made friends on the block. He's open, gentle. Ricky used to beat him up. Ricky's beat him up since he was a little boy. Now Jesus is bigger than Ricky. Last week he bashed Ricky's head against a wall. He tells me, "Ricky won't try nothing ever again." These days Ricky's on crack, not smack, so at least he's not dropping syringes out the window into the backyard, which was upsetting, watching needles fall on the garden.

'I wasn't sure if I were seeing slides or a film of the scene, it all happened so fast before my eyes. First Debbie ran forward and showed me the scars on her arms. That was awful. Then she tells me that her baby Jessica is one year old. She shows me Jessica's picture. Jessica is in Debbie's arms. The image is fuzzy and dark. Debbie's in pink and the child is looking up at her, smiling at her. I think it's a smile. Showing me the picture, Debbie is happy, as if the baby had not been taken away from her.'

So many stories. So many voices. All in need. In need of comfort. I am your comfort. I hold you. I let you go. I am true to you. I am a secret. I explain everything. I seduce you. You lose yourself. I am what you have lost. Your elusive past. Your fleeting present. Your irresistible and horrifying future. I am the little things in life. And the big things. I am lyrical. I am logical. I am steady. I am faithless. I am prosaic. I am poetic. I am hard. I am tender. I am the voice of reason. Of sanity. Of history. I will sing you an aria.

'No. I said no. And I said no again, and I said again, No, no, and I whispered No, and I sang No, and I screamed No, and then I said No, again, and again, and then I yelled No, never more, no, and no, and I hissed, No, then called out, No, then I murmured quietly, No, never, not again, no, and then, with more voice, shouted, No. No. No. No. Never. Never.'

I find it difficult to separate the beginning from the end, which makes it hard to record stories, to invent them, or erase them. This may be the end for Paige but stories go on and on and on, leading one into another relentlessly. There is no end to stories, they are without mercy. Still, you and I know stories that begin and end, as surely as you and I know that death comes to all things.

'We do not select the stories we write, we do not pick the voices. They take us by surprise and we surrender to them. They write us, they write in us, all over us, all through us. They occupy us. We are, in a sense, puppets – to language, with language.'

Not truly, not absolutely, not actually, not completely.

The night draws to a close, but it doesn't draw. The day dawns, but not for Paige. She is asleep, a small creature curled into the corner of her bed. She covers her head with a blanket. She burrows deeper into her dream. She dreams she has something wonderful to say and then she wakes up, and begins her day, first stopping the alarm clock, then making a cup of coffee, then looking for a shirt, then sitting at her desk. To find words. Paige wraps her hand around her neck and rubs her throat. She coughs and coughs.

NECK AND NECK

Zoë Fairbairns

DENISE

I realised something funny was going on, but that didn't mean it had to be another woman. Some wives might jump to that conclusion, but some wives are suspicious by nature. I happened to trust my husband.

What would he want another woman for? We had only been married for three years. We had everything. We had survived the war without any serious losses or injuries, we had found nice furnished rooms overlooking the park at £1.10sh a week, and, in spite of the fact that I thought we hadn't quite got the hang of the sex thing yet, I was expecting. Perhaps it was just me that hadn't got the hang of it. Of course with the baby on the way we'd had to give it up, but he didn't mind waiting. He said it would make him appreciate it all the more when normal service was resumed.

We didn't have a lot of money, but we had what we needed. Roy had come out of the army without any particular qualifications, but his common sense, strong arms and willingness to learn had got him taken on at a factory that made machinery for other factories. His wasn't a labouring job, nothing like that, more managerial. He was deputy to the man who was in charge of the supply store room. Roy checked deliveries in and requisitions out and made sure everything ended up where it was supposed to be.

Now he wasn't where he was supposed to be.

He was supposed to be staying at his mother's. It was his habit to work night shifts and odd hours and save his time off into a block so that he could pop up to the Midlands to make sure she was all right. I sometimes wished he and I could have more time together, but I told myself not to be selfish. She had brought him into the world and now he was all she had. And his devotion as a son boded well for what kind of father he would be to our child, and what kind of husband to me in years to come when my youthful bloom might start to get a bit tarnished.

So there he was staying at his mother's, or rather there he wasn't, because here was this telegram, addressed to him from a hospital in her home town. REGRET YOUR MOTHER SERIOUSLY ILL COME IMMEDIATELY.

For his sake I tried hard to mind more about his mother being ill, but I couldn't. She was elderly, and I had only met her twice. She had not been particularly friendly. If she died I would have more of Roy. Only where was Roy? Why had the hospital sent him a telegram about his mother being ill when they could have told him personally because he was staying with her?

In the middle of the night, another telegram arrived. REGRET YOUR MOTHER HAS PASSED AWAY.

He was due home the following day. I went to meet him at the railway station. I had no plans about what I was going to say or do. My mind was blank. I knew there was a perfectly simple explanation. I just hadn't come up with it yet.

I saw him before he saw me. He didn't look as if he had been in any sort of trouble. He looked as he always looked: well-dressed and well-groomed, without being fussy or un-masculine. He was strong-looking and stocky with broad shoulders, glossy chestnut hair and warm brown eyes. In the corner of his mouth was a freshly lit Park Drive with a filter tip. He was wearing what he had gone away in: his light grey summer suit with his silk hanky in his breast pocket, and his straw boater with the narrow brim. He carried his things in the brown suitcase that he got when he was demobbed.

I flung myself clumsily towards him and hugged him till my arms ached. He dropped his cigarette, ground it underfoot and returned my hug. It was enough. I didn't need to know where he had been, and I never would need to know. All that mattered was that he had come back from wherever it was and would never have to leave me again because his reason for leaving me — his mother — was dead.

I should have left it at that. But I had to be clever. 'How was your mother?' I asked, all innocence.

'Fine.' He lit another cigarette. 'Soldiering on.'

'Wonderful, isn't she?' I observed. 'For her age.'

'Sends her love.'

'That's very kind of her.' I spoke slowly. I paused. I gave him five seconds, one more chance to change his story. He didn't change it. He stayed silent. He looked quizzical. We faced each other over his lie which lay like a fat, grey maggot, bursting with — what? Poison? Contempt? The contempt he must feel for me and for his mother, to be able to lie about her to me. I swooped on the lie like a sharp-beaked bird. 'Clever of her to send anything, being as she's dead.' I seemed to feel the soft grub writhing in its death-throes under the prod of my beak. It tasted bitter.

He said, 'What do you mean, Denise?'

'What do *you* mean by lying to me? Where have you been?'

'Never mind that,' he said, staring. 'Tell me about Mum.'

'I'll tell you nothing until you tell me where you've been! You weren't with her, were you? Who were you with?'

His face had gone grey. He gripped my elbow with sharp fingers. He looked round as if he feared we were being spied upon.

'You don't want to know,' he said.

'I insist on knowing, damn you!'

'Let's get inside, then,' he said.

We had reached the house. I felt like barring his way. I didn't want him in our home. But where was he to go? What was I to do? Watch him leave, then make my solitary way up the stairs to our rooms and live alone among his things? Or throw them after him and live without them, without him? My baby moved warningly. *What about me? Me, me, me?*

We went into our kitchen. He put his hat on the table and sat and smoked. He said, 'What about Mum?'

I said, 'Roy, I'm waiting.'

He said, 'If you force me to tell you, don't you reproach me afterwards.'

'There's nothing you can tell me that's worse than what I've imagined.'

'Don't be so sure,' he said.

'I am sure.'

'I wasn't at Mum's because I was at a hanging.'

'Hanging what?'

'A man.'

'What are you talking about, Roy?'

'My job.'

'You're a warehouse under-manager.'

'I'm a hangman.'

ROY

Don't blame me. What else could I have said?

It wasn't my fault.

Well, all right, fair enough, I suppose it was my fault for breaking my marriage vows in the first place and going off for a few days with old Annabel, giving Denise my usual line that I was going to Mum's. But you show me a married man who never went against the letter of the law and I'll show you a pansy.

Denise was a lovely girl. Little and bouncy, with curly black hair and a sweet nature, and just enough of a temper simmering there to keep you in line and keep life interesting. Good cook, careful housekeeper. Always nicely turned out, and even that didn't cost me a fortune because she made her clothes herself. Any man would be proud to show her off as his wife. She just wasn't very sexy, that's all. Some women aren't. It's nobody's fault. It's the way they're made, some of them. There's a lot to be said for it. It made her sort of special, if you know what I mean. A safe little garden to grow my son in. A walled garden. I knew I didn't have to worry about what she was up to when I was away.

She wasn't interested in that side of marriage. She didn't want it. Even when she wanted it she didn't *really* want it. And I was the last man to impose myself where I was not wanted. Annabel, though, she really wanted it. Wanted me. Where I'm wanted, I go. What harm is there in that?

There needn't have been any harm in it, if Mum hadn't had one of her turns and died just when I needed her. Not that I blame her, but it did rather throw me on to the wrong foot. I loved my mum, and when Denise gave me the news that she was dead, all out of the blue and without any build-up, I wasn't my own man. You've only got one mother, and she only has one death, and that's quite enough for a man to deal with without his wife wanting to know where he's been and what he's been doing. Particularly when he's been doing precisely what a woman has in mind when she asks those sorts of question.

So I said the first thing that came into my head. I happened to know there'd been a hanging that week and I said I'd done it. Me, hanging a man by the neck until he was dead. I get squeamish if I try to set a mouse trap.

Denise was obviously thinking the same thing. 'You? The hangman?' '*A* hangman,' I said cautiously. 'Not *the*.' I'd never taken an interest in the subject up till now, and for all I knew the hangman — the real one — was a household name. I wasn't a household name and I couldn't start being one. I was in enough trouble as it was. 'There's more than one,' I explained.

'Why?' she demanded.

I looked at her hurt, questioning little eyes and her clenched fists and I thought, Roy, my old mate, give up. You're never going to get away with this, so admit the truth, throw yourself on her mercy, promise never to see Annabel again and start afresh. Denise is a good girl — better than you deserve — and she'll have you back, if you make a clean breast of it, now. *Now*.

'Why?' said Denise again.

For some reason I thought she meant. *Why Annabel*?

She couldn't have meant that because she didn't know about Annabel, but I had had a tiring few days. I knew only too well why Annabel. I needed her. It was a sex thing. Annabel knew that as well as I did, that was what made it such a good arrangement. I couldn't give her up just like that. I needed time to think.

'Why?' Denise repeated, so loudly that the neighbours

would be in any minute. I had to answer, but what was the question again? Ah yes – why is there more than one hangman?

Well. Why would there be?

I improvised. 'Because it takes more than one man to hang another man, Denise.' I dared say it did, especially if the one who was being hanged was awkward about it. 'And of course you have to have reserves.' It seemed a safe sort of guess. The army had reserves, football teams had reserves, actors had understudies, so why should hangmen be any different? 'In case one of them – one of us, that is – is indisposed. Or otherwise engaged.'

'I don't care how many there are. I meant why are you one of them?'

'Somebody's got to do it,' I said.

'Why's it got to be you?'

I shrugged. 'It's not everybody's cup of tea. Talking of which – shall I make us one?'

DENISE

It took a bit of getting used to. But as he said, somebody's got to do it. And whoever that somebody is, chances are he's going to have a wife.

So there was no point in feeling sorry for myself and saying 'why me?' Why not me? I had married him for better or for worse. And there were worse things in the world than hangmen.

People who get sentenced to be hanged, for one thing. Not fit to live in the first place, most of them. Imagine waking up one morning and finding you're married to somebody like that. Or imagine – and Roy put this to me one day a few months after Elizabeth was born, while I was still trying to get used to the idea of Roy's, well, job — imagine waking up one morning and finding that one of those sub-human creatures had hurt your child. 'Hurt one hair on little Lizzie's head, Denise. Wouldn't you want to do what I do to them? Wouldn't you do it? If you could lay your hands on them?'

'I would, Roy.'

'But you'll never have to, Denise. And neither will any other member of the British public, bar a handful of us who've made it our calling. The rest of you can sleep easy in your beds, knowing that side of things is taken care of.'

'Roy — '

'What, love?'

'Can I — help in any way?'

He looked horrified, but I hadn't mean it in a morbid way. I wasn't offering to go to the scaffold with him. Whatever my brave words about what I would do to someone who hurt Lizzie, I knew I wouldn't really dare, even if it were allowed. I was the sort who felt squeamish if I had to set a mouse trap. So was Roy, funnily enough. What I had meant was more to do with the wives of other important men having a rôle to play. Doctors' wives answered the phone and sent flowers to the bereaved, coal miners' wives washed their husbands' pit clothes, and the wives of Members of Parliament opened garden fêtes. 'I'd like to do something.'

'The best help you can give me,' he said, 'is to pretend I never told you.'

'All right, Roy. I'll try.'

ROY

When I first told Annabel what excuse I'd given Denise for not being where I was supposed to be, she said, 'That's the best one I've ever heard.'

I thought, *best of how many?* but I didn't say it. The question would not have been appreciated. I knew the rules. I didn't make difficulties about Annabel's other boy friends and she didn't make difficulties about Denise.

Annabel made jokes instead. 'You're well hung, I'll say that for you.' 'Don't keep me in suspense.' 'If you carry on like that, you're going to be for the high jump.'

And then there was the letter. It arrived one morning when I was having breakfast sitting opposite Denise, with little Lizzie messing up her cereal on the tray of her high chair. It was in a plain brown envelope with the address typed, I thought it was from the income tax. But it seemed to be from the governor of a prison.

> Dear Sir,
> The appeal of the prisoner named below has been dismissed and the High Sheriff of the County has fixed the undermentioned date for the execution.
>
> I am forwarding a Railway Warrant for your journey and I shall be glad if you will report to the prison not later than 4 p.m. on the day before. Accommodation will be provided for you.
>
> Will you please acknowledge receipt of the Railway Warrant and confirm that you can accept this engagement. A stamped addressed envelope is enclosed for your reply.
>
> Yours faithfully.

I nearly had a heart attack. I mean, rationally I recognised the hand of Annabel and her warped sense of humour, but this letter had my name and address on it and I wasn't being completely rational. I really felt as if I were being called to put a man to death.

Denise said, 'What's that, Roy?'

'Business.' I put the letter away and glanced significantly at our daughter to warn Denise that, young though she was, you never knew what she was taking in. Denise changed the subject.

I took the first opportunity to give Annabel absolute hell. 'What do you think you're playing at?'

'I thought you'd be pleased,' she said.

'Where did you get that bloody thing?'

'Never you mind.'

'It's got my name and address on it,' I said.

'Look again,' she said.

Someone else's name and address had been rubbed out and mine typed over. It was a neat job, I wouldn't have noticed.

'Give it back to me and it can be our code,' said Annabel. 'I can send it to you as a signal that I fancy a spot of necking.' And she went off into peals of laughter.

I didn't like this. I was starting to feel diminished by the whole business. I kept thinking of how my sex life was at the mercy not only of judges, juries and the criminal classes, but Annabel too. I didn't like the idea of only being summoned when she felt like it. What about me? When I wanted her, I wanted her. Still, what I had was better than nothing.

'It's difficult for me, Roy,' said Denise one day.

'What is?'

'When you take your days off from the factory and go off, and there's a hanging on the wireless what am I supposed to think? What am I supposed to tell people, come to that? I can't exactly say you've gone to your mother's, can I?'

'Good point, Denise.'

'Roy.'

'What?'

'How did you get into this?'

'Into what?'

'What we're talking about.'

I said, 'It's something I picked up in the army. After that – well, friend of a friend, word of mouth, you know how these things work.'

'No I don't,' she said. 'And what are we going to tell Elizabeth her dad is?'

'Warehouse under-manager.' Ask a silly question.

She put her hands on her hips. 'Warehouse under-manager who disappears for three or four days every time there's a hanging on the wireless.'

'I see your point, Denise.'

'Elizabeth's not to know anything about it. We must spare her.'

'Yes,' I said.

Denise gritted her teeth. 'What I am getting at is that before she starts sitting up and taking notice I think you need a change of job. You need something where you'll be away from home anyway – '

'What's his name?' I joked.

'What's whose name?'

'The fancy man you want me out of the way for.'

'Don't be disgusting. You need some sort of travelling job where you'll be away from home anyway from time to time.'

'What did you have in mind, Denise?'

'Something like this.' She showed me an advertisement that she had marked in the paper. *The Manufacturers of Lady Clara Chocolate Superiors are looking for respectable gentlemen of good appearance to sell their product to discerning retail outlets. Must be available to travel throughout the United Kingdom.*

'Perfect for you, Roy, I've always said you're cut out for something better than factory work. Now when you go away Elizabeth won't notice anything special about it, and I won't have to either.'

'If that's what you want, love,' I sighed. I let her remind me a couple of times before I got round to sending in the application. I didn't want to look too keen.

It was easy money at Lady Clara Chocolate Superiors. Superior was the word; those chocolates sold themselves, more or less. In a typical week, I'd be away from home maybe two or three nights. That's between eight and twelve overnight stays per month. Some of those overnight stays were to do with my work selling chocolates. I'd be chasing up new customers, keeping the old ones happy and staying on my own in cheap hotels. Other nights, I'd be doing pleasanter things.

ELIZABETH

Dear Sir,
The appeal of the above named has been dismissed and the High Sheriff of the County has fixed the undermentioned date for the execution . . .

'Mummy.'

She's standing at the sink with her back to me, washing Daddy's shirts. She doesn't turn round. 'Yes, Elizabeth?'

'What does this say?'

'What does what say?'

'This word. A — p — p — '

She turns and takes the piece of paper out of my hands. Her wet soapy fingers make marks. 'Where did you get this?'

'I found it.'

'*Where?*'

I don't answer because I don't know. I've forgotten. It was lying about and it looked as if it would be a good piece of paper for me to draw pictures on. When I noticed writing on the back I tried to read the words.

I seem to be in trouble for it, but I don't see why, I thought she liked it when I tried to read. I thought they both liked it. I thought they liked me to ask them about difficult words. But she is shouting: 'You must never, never, never look at grown-up people's private correspondence!'

'What does private correspondence mean?'

'How much of it have you read?'

'I can't read it! I don't know what that word is! A – p – p – '

'Apple,' she says, folding the letter away into her apron pocket. 'The word is apple.'

'Apple.'

'Do you want an apple now?'

'Yes, please.'

She peels me one and slices it. It's hard and sour and I can't chew it properly. It gets stuck in my throat. I cough. I can't breathe. My neck is blocked. My mother pats my back, strokes my neck. She gives me a drink of water to help the apple down. It creeps down the inside of my neck like a man going down a ladder, one-step, two-step, three-step, four-step, down into my insides.

She takes me on her lap. She hugs me. 'There!' I rest against her, but I haven't forgotten about the letter. She thinks I have, but I haven't. I can feel it in the pocket of her apron. Through the fabric, against the side of my neck, I feel crinkled up paper. It's the letter she hid. The secret letter, I know there's a secret about that letter. I could tell from her eyes when she read it.

I can remember what each word of the letter looks like. I've got pictures of them in my mind. I can't read the letter, but I'll be able to one day. In the meantime I've got pictures of the shapes of all the words. Shapes that mean something. I'll keep the shapes in my memory until I'm old enough to read the words and know what they mean. Old enough to know the secret.

I go to school now. I can't read yet but I like sums. We've got a shop in our class. We learn how to pay for things and give change.

We have Lady Clara Chocolate Superiors in the shop, from Daddy. Daddy is a commercial traveller. He taught me how to say that on my first day at school. 'If anyone asks you what your Daddy's job is,' he said, 'say, "he travels in Lady Clara Chocolate Superiors."'

Outside our classroom shop stands Lady Clara herself. She isn't a real lady. She's as tall as a real lady but she is made of cardboard. She has a nice smile and a frilly cardboard dress down to her ankles but if you look behind her you can see that she is flat and brown. She is propped up on a stick, otherwise she would fall over. Daddy gave her to us.

The chocolates she offers are only pretend. She wants you to come into the shop and buy some real ones. Daddy stands like that when he says goodbye to me before he goes away on his long journeys to sell chocolates. He makes me laugh so that I won't cry. I always cry when Daddy goes away. I don't like our house without him. It's quiet and sad. Mummy won't let me have the wireless on. She says she wants a bit of peace and quiet for a change.

Daddy says if I cry when he goes away he'll cry as well and that would never do. He twirls his umbrella like Lady

Clara's parasol and tips his hat to the back of his head like her bonnet. He makes his voice go high like a lady's voice and he says: 'Lady Clara calling!'

'Don't go, Daddy!'

'I've got to, sweetheart. Otherwise there won't be enough sweets in the shops for all the good children. Are there any good children here for me to give sweets to?'

'Me, me, me!'

He opens his case. It's full of tiny chocolate bars wrapped in different coloured silver paper and cellophane. Samples. I am allowed to choose.

Mummy says, 'You'll ruin your teeth, Elizabeth! Keep some for your friends at school. Don't eat them all.' But I want to eat them all. Why shouldn't I eat them all? They're mine. They're from Daddy, for me. I gobble all I can, filling myself with the sweet hope of Daddy's return.

At school, Lady Clara holds out her box of chocolates. You can't eat them because they're made of chalk and glued down. They would gum up your throat. They would get stuck in your neck and choke you, like that bit of apple. *The word is apple.* Was it? We have cards in class with pictures of apples and marks underneath that the teacher says mean 'apple' but they aren't the same marks as the one on the letter I found. I don't think they are. I can't be sure because I can't read. But I remember what that letter looked like. The letter that Mummy got so upset about me seeing that she hid it in her apron pocket.

The picture of the letter is fading from my mind. It's sinking out of sight like a piece of paper falling down a well. Floating down the air and sinking through the water. I can barely make out the shapes of the words. I want to hold on to them until I can recognise their shapes, read them, know the secret, understand. I want to know what the words mean. I think they are something to do with Daddy going away. If I understood them, he wouldn't go away. He goes away because I am bad. Because I can't read. I wish I could read, but I am afraid. I want to know the secret but it might be bad. I want to remember what the words looked like in the secret letter but I don't want to know about the badness.

In class we sing 'Ding dong bell, pussy's in the well'. There's a picture on the wall to go with the song. Underneath the picture are black marks which are words which say 'ding dong bell'. I know they say that because the teacher told me.

If I could learn to read, I would know why the pussy is in the well. Dropped in by the scruff of her neck and falling, falling. I would understand about the bell. Ding dong bell, is it a clock? Is there a particular time for dropping pussies down wells? Do they say, *come along, pussy, it's time now*? Does the pussy plead for five more minutes like me at bed-time? I want to know but I can't read. The shapeless black words hover round the picture like crows.

I get given special books but I still can't read so I get dumped in a special class with a special teacher and a lot of backward boys.

I'm not backward. I've heard the teachers say that when they discuss me as if I'm not there. 'It's not as if Elizabeth is backward. There's nothing wrong with her arithmetic, her speech, her physical co-ordination, her perception and comprehension skills. And she comes from a good home.'

Back at the good home, my parents take up the chorus only more loudly. '*Why can't you read*? Bringing shame on us. We've no patience with this dyslexia business, we didn't have dyslexia in our day. A girl who couldn't read would be sat at the back of the kindergarten, big though she was, year in, year out, until she damn well could read! Try, Elizabeth.

You're just not trying.'

They were the stupid ones, if they thought I didn't try. Did they think I didn't want to be normal? I pretended I didn't care whether I could read or not and maybe the reason why they got so angry was that I fooled them into thinking I didn't care, but I didn't fool myself. I wanted to read all right. Quite apart from not liking being at the bottom of the class when I knew I belonged at the top, reading looked interesting, it looked fun, and anyway what would become of me if I couldn't read? Who would employ me, who would want to marry me if I couldn't read to our children? How would my children respect me if they could read and I couldn't? Why wouldn't I want to read? Was it my fault if all letters merged together looked the same as if I were looking at them through darkness even in the middle of the day? I tried to explain about the darkness. They sent me for eye tests. They said my eyesight was normal.

'Elizabeth, you are perfectly normal. You are of above average intelligence. You must be able to see that an "a" is different from a "p".' I lost patience. 'All right,' I said, 'you say I must be able to, so I can. But I sodding can't. Sodding a's and sodding p's still look the sodding same to me and so do all the other sodding letters. And if I'm of above average intelligence what am I doing here among all you cretins?' Here ended my school career.

My parents and the Youth Employment found me a job in insurance. They said there were prospects. Sure there were. I took tea round the Life Office. Death Office was more like it. I couldn't read anything though one day I thought I recognised 'Dear Sir' and anyway I overheard what they were doing. I couldn't believe that anyone would do such a thing. They sat there with tables of figures working out when their customers were going to die. It turned me right off. I mean who wants to know exactly when they're going to die? What a torture, waiting for it to happen. Also this was round about the time when Dad died suddenly of a heart attack on one of his business trips so that sort of got to me. Not that he'd known he was going to die. Off he'd gone as usual to sell his chocolates and the next thing Mum knew she was being called to collect his body from a hotel bedroom.

I was falsely accused of smashing up the Life Office for being a Death Office so I left. There were other jobs but I didn't last. They always want you to read. They want you to talk, too. Talking's another thing of mine that I've started to have difficulty with. It's quite awkward.

It started when I met up again with Alf from my remedial reading class. He's not remedial any more, nothing like it, he's got his own cosmetics business. I help him with packaging and thinking up slogans. I told him I've got selling in my blood, what with Dad being such a success with Lady Clara Chocolate Superiors that they even used to send him abroad. Anyway, I thought up this slogan to go with Alf's Neck Moisturising and Anti-Wrinkle Soap. 'A beautiful neck is every woman's rightful possession. Slender, elegant and blemish free, it is the thoroughfare between her head and her heart.' Soon after that I started getting this lump in my throat and not being able to talk through it.

It's a cross between laryngitis, food going down the wrong way and feeling very, very frightened. But why should I be frightened? Alf's like a brother. He massages my shoulders to help me relax. He says why don't I move in and then he'll massage all of me, all day, every day.

The trouble is, I don't like it when he touches my neck. I panic: 'Don't touch my neck!'

He says, 'Has someone hurt your neck?'

I want to say, 'It's my thoroughfare and it's blocked,' but

it would sound silly. And anyway, I've got a lump in my throat, I can't speak.

DENISE

I've seen everything now. Is nothing sacred? A hangman's widow on *The Gary Hindlesham Show*. A woman like me. No, not like me. I wouldn't insult my husband's memory by talking about him on *The Gary Hindlesham Show*, or on any other television programme.

I've nothing against *The Gary Hindlesham Show*. On the contrary, in the normal way it's the high point of my week, leading the lonely life I lead now that Elizabeth has chosen to go and live with that strange young man. She's a grown woman, I suppose she knows her own mind. I'm just glad her father isn't here to see it.

To a person of my generation, television is still a miracle, and *The Gary Hindlesham Show* is like having a little party in your own front room that you don't have to bother to do the cheese straws for.

Not that I'd invite a woman like that to any party of mine. The so-called widow of the so-called hangman. She's written a book, that's why she's on. A book about her husband! What happened to confidentiality? What happened to professional discretion and good taste? What happened to the Official Secrets Act?

The time limit's lapsed, apparently. People are free to write books. I don't suppose she wrote it herself. Doesn't look the type who could string two sentences together.

She'd be better occupied keeping her two legs together. Look at the way she's sitting in her mutton-dressed-up-as-lamb frock. Listen to her, reducing the whole thing to a floor show. 'It was like anything else, Gary. Like wallpapering a room. Preparation was the secret. Preparation, professionalism and attention to detail. Everything had to be oiled, checked, weighed and measured. You had to get it right. The thing to aim for was an instantaneous fracture dislocation between the second and third vertebrae. What those people didn't realise, Gary, who went and had it abolished, was that provided you got it right, death was instantaneous. Bob's your uncle, just like that. Hardly a punishment at all really.'

She sounds as if she resents the people who got it abolished. That's probably because abolition meant the end of her husband's working life. It didn't mean that for Roy. If anything he was called away more often after abolition than before. For test runs and training and maintaining the equipment just in case. And then of course he became a consultant to various foreign governments. Always flying off here, there and everywhere. He never took me with him, though I begged him to, but he always brought me back lots of duty frees. We told Elizabeth that he'd been away on business, which of course he had. That's probably what killed him in the end. Jet-lag in the service of humanity.

Gary Hindlesham is saying. 'You say death was instantaneous as long as he got it right. How often *did* he get it right?'

'My husband? Every time. I can't speak for the others.'

'What others?'

'Assistants. Reserves. Number Two's. Call them what you like. We didn't associate more than was strictly necessary. They weren't a very nice sort of person, and nobody appreciated that more than the prisoners. Hardened men used to beg and plead to have my husband do it rather than one of the riff-raff. Not so far removed from the criminal element themselves.'

'How many were there?' Gary asks.

She winks. 'Not as many as some women thought.'

'What do you mean by that?'

She smirks. 'My old man was the real thing but he had imitators.'

'*Imitators*?'

'Don't worry, love, they didn't actually do it.' She pats Gary's knee. 'Least, I hope not. They'd've got it wrong, hadn't had the training, see? They had other things on their minds.'

'What other things?'

'Don't come the Mr Innocent with me, Gary. Don't you men like to get away from the wife now and again?' She unfolds a piece of paper. 'You'd be surprised,' she says, 'how much he could sell one of these letters for, on the black market. Some of them went to museums of criminology and bona-fide collectors, but not all by a long chalk.'

She spreads out the letter and the camera moves in close.

> Dear Sir,
> The appeal of the prisoner named below has been dismissed and the High Sheriff of the County has fixed the undermentioned date for the execution.

I look away, but I can't escape the sound of her voice. 'Be honest, Gary. Wouldn't you pay a bit for an alibi like that, to spend a night or two with the girlfriend, no questions asked?'

ELIZABETH

It's like a cell of a honeycomb. I wait in the cell, naked as a grub, except for the light white robe they made me put on.

On the wall of the cell is a notice which of course I can't read.

'What does that say?' I croak, when they come for me. I need every scrap of information. 'I haven't got my glasses.'

'"Please tell the radiographer if you are or might be pregnant."'

'If I am, does that mean you won't do it?'

'We might have to postpone it. Does it apply in your case?'

'No. Might as well get it over with.'

Another door opens in the cubicle, the cell. I didn't realise there were two doors, one for coming in, one for going out. The cell is a thoroughfare, blocked by me. And I am blocked by – what? A cell? No one's mentioned cancer yet. That worries me. I saw Jack Hawkins in a film after he had his throat taken out. He talked through a hole in his neck. It didn't sound like talking.

I am led forward into darkness. They make me stand on a line drawn on the floor in front of a screen. I wait while they get ready. I'm so alone, in my white robe and bare feet.

They give me barium. It looks like a milk shake and tastes like chalk. Pretend white chocolate, melted. Lady Clara Chocolate Superiors, pretend ones that you couldn't swallow or they'd gum up your throat. I'm solid with forced-down chocolate. They take X-rays of my neck from different angles with the barium slithering down. I watch my transparent neck on the screen. My larynx. They'll take it away. It will serve me right for claiming my neck and all that goes through it – what I swallow, what I speak – as my rightful possessions. They are not.

All those little backbones greenly glowing. Tough and delicate, brittle but braced to hold me together. Hold my head on. Bigger and bigger as they burrow into my body, smaller and smaller as they soar into my head.

There's something on the X-ray. They won't say what but they admit me at once for exploratory surgery first thing tomorrow morning, so it's pretty obvious. My last meal is a bowl of soup and a sleeping pill. In the middle of the night a nurse comes tiptoeing in and takes away my water jug. She puts a sign on my bed: NIL BY MOUTH. From now on I eat through a hole in my neck.

'We'll give you a little prick in your bottom, and then you'll feel relaxed and happy.'

'I'd call it a vicious stab rather than a little prick but it sets me singing. Me! Singing without a voice. '*Ding, dong bell, pussy's in the well.* Don't mind if I sing, do you?'

'Feel free, Elizabeth.' They mean, *Sing while you can. Ding dong bell.*

'We're taking you to theatre now, Elizabeth.'

'Okay.'

Doesn't matter to them whether I say okay or not okay, I'm helpless as a drowned kitten, my neck flopping. Hangdog, hangkitten, hangpussies in the well.

'Feeling sleepy yet, Elizabeth?'

No, not a bit, I feel absolutely . . .

Down.

Down, down, down into the well.

The long dark tube, drain-pipe, pot-hole, inside my own neck, my thoroughfare. They're going down my throat with a torch and a camera and a knife but I have nothing to aid me in my lonely descent to my depths, nothing to keep me company, nothing, no one.

Only this gleam of white light. A hole in my neck to let in daylight? No, a sheet of paper fly-posted to the inside wall of the well like a wanted poster, 'Dear Sir . . .'

The letter that I couldn't read. I made a picture of it in my mind when I was little and hid the picture away for when I would be big. But I lost it and I never became big enough to read. I wasn't brave enough. Now, alone at the bottom of the depths of my well, I know what it says. I thought I'd lost the letter but it was here all along, down here, fly-posted to the inside of my insides, waiting for me to be brave enough to come down and read it. Down here I can read. 'The appeal . . .' not *apple*, it never was *apple*, '. . . of the prisoner named below has been dismissed and the High Sheriff of the County has fixed the undermentioned date for the execution . . .'

'Elizabeth! Wake up! You've had your operation.'

Yes, yes, but what's left of me? Is there a hole in my neck, is there apple in my throat?

'It wasn't cancer,' they say, using the word for the first time.

'What was it?'

'A laryngeal oedema.'

'What?'

'A fluid-filled cyst on your voice box. It's not serious, it's probably an allergy, we can cure it with pills.'

A fluid-filled cyst, blocking my voice.

Water from my well.

Ding dong bell.

When Alf comes in at visiting time I tell him: 'I dreamed my father was the public hangman.'

'Probably that horrible old cow on the box. Giving you nightmares.'

'What old cow?'

'On the Gary thingy show. Said she used to be married to a hangman. He used to flog his official letters to other blokes so that they could use them as an excuse to go off for a few days with the fancy woman.'

'How revolting.'

It is revolting, but not as revolting as being a hangman.

He stuffed my throat with chocolate to distract me from what he was doing to other people's throats. But what was he doing? Throttling or caressing?

I'd rather it was caressing.

DENISE

I wonder how much that woman on *The Gary Hindlesham Show* got paid for saying those terrible things? Mind you, it didn't surprise me to hear that her husband sold his official correspondence for cash, so that others could make dishonest use of it.

Roy wouldn't have even contemplated such a thing. I'm sure in my own mind that if I went through his things I would find every single letter of appointment intact and in mint condition.

I could take them to the newspaper library and match up dates of letters with dates of executions and names of prisons and they would all be correct. I could probably even check with the Home Office, now that the Official Secrets time limit has elapsed, and they would confirm that my husband was what he said he was and went where he said he went.

I could do all these things but I'm not going to. That is the sort of thing mistrustful wives might do. Not me. Life's too short to go sniffing suspiciously about. Life *is* short, and it's about time Elizabeth knew the truth about her father. It would make it feel that bit truer if she knew. We spared her the truth, we thought we were sparing her, but maybe one of the reasons why she's had these little difficulties in her life is that she hasn't had the chance to admire him. So I've decided to tell her. She's a grown woman, she's entitled to be proud, as I am. And her pride will be further proof that it was all true, true that he wasn't just *a* hangman, he was *the* hangman. He was professional and skilful, hardened criminals begged for it to be him, it was hardly a punishment at all really. Experts came from miles around to admire his fracture dislocations. He was an expert consultant to foreign governments. He was the hangman and I was the hangman's helpmeet. We were a team, Roy, Elizabeth and I. Somebody had to do it, and it was us.

The passive condition of womankind is subject unto more diseases and of other sortes and nature then men are . . . But amongst all the diseases whereunto that sex is obnoxious, there is none comparable unto this which is called The Suffocation of the Mother, either for varietie, or for strangeness of accidents. . . . I say of the Mother or wombe because although the wombe many times in this disease doe suffer but secondarily, yet the other parts are not affected in this disease but of the Mother . . . which finding itselfe annoyed by some unkind humor, either within it selfe, or in the vessels adjoining or belonging unto it, doth by a naturall instinct which is ingrafted in every part of the body for his own preservation, endevour to expell that which is offensive: in which conflict if either the passage be obstructed, or the humor inobedient or malignant, or the functions of the wombe any way depraved, the offence is communicated from thence unto the rest of the body . . . as the stomacke, entrailess, vaines, spleen, & c. . . . These parts are affected in this disease, and do suffer in their functions as they are diminished, depraved, or abolished, according to the nature and plenty of the humor, and the temperament and situation of the Mother.

Jorden, *Of The Suffocation of the Mother*

'. . . *beware of fainting fits . . . Though at the time they maybe refreshing & Agreeable yet beleive me they will in the end, if too often repeated & at improper seasons, proves destructive to your Constitution . . . A frenzy fit is not one quarter so pernicious; . . . Run mad as often as you chuse; but do not faint.*'

Jane Austen, *Love and Friendship*

BELLY CRY

Nicole Ward Jouve

'You mustn't cry,' she told herself, 'you'll just make him miserable. And the drive ahead. Mustn't crash. So easy to do.' Route 2. The long American car swimming into the sunset.

Whilst your son caught a plane and flew eastwards over the ocean.

Your eyes swimming. Or was it the rain, spattering, streaking the glass panels of the terminal. Streaming. The dark glass dome arching over you like a huge bubble. An aquarium: but the water was outside.

You were called Anna.

'You'll have to be very courageous,' her husband had told her that other time. Over a year ago now. Felt like yesterday. He'd been so uncharacteristically, so exquisitely, kind. A miracle, she'd thought. He'd been cutting wood. She'd been out. When she'd come in, there were several letters on the sofa. For her. They looked interesting. Normally he would have been ratty: all the mail for her. No sense in pointing out to him that she wrote lots of letters, kept in touch with lots of people. He saw the mail she got, his own absence of it, as one more of her plots against him. Out to take it all away from him. And now she was writing about female murderers. It all went to show, didn't it? She was out to murder him. Out out out. She apologized, she belittled herself. We both know, she hinted, you're the one. She knew, she didn't have to hint, that at bottom she was no good. Trammelled by a hundred obligations and confusions. Keep quiet. Don't rock the boat. Listen to what they're really saying, the father, the husband, listen to the thing that speaks behind, under, the words of aggression, the words of anger. Your father's will to power rooted in his own frailty. Threatened by chaos, has to have order, rule the roost. Despotic yes, but can you teach new tricks to an old dog? It's his house after all, if he wants order, if he wants silence, meals dead on time, it's his right. If he needs you to listen to his views on politics, and you don't agree, what's the point of arguing? It'll just make him angry, you'll get angry yourself, upset. Better be patient, better be mature. The good daughter. And your husband's temper, like milk. Boils over, spills over, 'You stupid bitch, I'm driving, and you can't even find the road! You've lived here all your life. Right or left?' God I don't know.

'Left,' she says, thinking there's a fifty per cent chance. She might be the good thief, she might end up in heaven. It might be the right road. If not. Well, we'll survive.

He'll calm down, there'll be a joke, a gesture of affection. He's so sweet at bottom. Just take it. Don't you rage. For Pete's sake (for she doesn't swear, how could Christ protect her if she took his name in vain when she prays to him?), for Pete's sake (surely Saint Peter could take it, he was one of the disciples, he ended up crucified upside down, didn't think he was worthy to be crucified the right way up, like his master, his master's voice), for Pete's sake, woman, act grown up. You can take it.

Protect your son. Pretend everything is all right. Pretend your brother has not died, a year ago is it, and you don't know how to survive that death. Pretend your uncle, your mother's brother, did not die the year before, and that seeing your mother's grief – a brother, then a son – you don't now fear that your own son might be next in line, that the son is bound to follow in the brother's footsteps. Oh death the all-powerful the invisible, are you in here, in this airport's dark bubble, or out there, streaming?

No no. Pretend. Pretend your husband, now on the other side of the Atlantic, in Bristol, visiting your parents, has not just had this terrible row with them. And now your son is returning home, home to his father in London, and your mother was sobbing on the telephone, and you are trying to smother the roving, welling thing at the pit of your stomach. But oh no, everything will be all right, just pretend. Bad enough as it is, a mother like you. A bundle of nerves. An intellectual. A job. A woman who writes books. Who sees ghosts of fear. Fear is her lord. Hopeless as a mother, really. Up in the clouds, out of the house. Least you can do is not involve your son. Not create, so he won't get caught in the whirlwind. Reassure. Shut up. Give them space.

Like a bad taste in the mouth after a meal that's risen, condensed into nightmare, the night overcast oh, night so dark. A dark cloud compacted of ocean drops, it broods over the face of the waters. It will not break, you sweat. A mess, her writing: belly.

He could be so sweet. That time, he had been so sweet. He had come into the house, leant his axe against the wall. His eyes were green were light, like that time when she'd come in terror to tell him it was no good, they had no future together, he scared her, they were too different: and there would be freedom, the end of this oppression, the fear in her belly, the taste of fear in her mouth. Fear fear oh fear all her life, the fear of men was it, the fear of sex. When she was a little child, she'd been so hysterically afraid of dogs. This child's throwing a hysterical fit, they said, the grown-ups. Control yourself, they said. You can do it. Her father had bought her a medal of Saint Christopher. She was seven, she could read. There was Saint Christopher carrying the child on his shoulders, and on the reverse, 'One look at Saint Christopher and your fear will go away.' Magic, she'd thought. The relief, oh the relief. All she would have to do would be grab the medal, look at Saint Christopher, and — no fear, oh what delight what wonder. She could still remember, how old was she now, no need to say, I'll remember all my life: she had. The tall grass, the flowers in the hay, the scent of hay and the insects in the halo of the sun, and on the path the dog. The terror, the scramble for Daddy's arms, lift me up please, and then the thought, of course the medal. Its tongue was hanging out, it was panting, its saliva dribbled, the fangs were wet. And I'll huff and I'll puff and I'll blow your house down. Brown, the dog was brown. The medal the medal. She'd grabbed the medal. And. Looked at it: maybe it takes time. She'd held the medal. Please please. Nothing. Fear raced through her limbs, its root in her belly, her hands her feet shook from this thing so deep, shook shook, oh to be like the child perched up there on Saint Christopher's shoulders! Daddy Daddy. She clung to his trouser legs, he had her little brother up in his arms, 'you're a big girl' and her mother, the sternness, 'child, pull yourself together'. Make it go away, oh make it go away.

That was the terrible thing about dogs. The grown-ups

never understood. They were so big, they were something else, and they kept coming. Almost as if they could smell your fear, they smelt that you would be afraid, the one who'd be afraid, and they came for you. There could have been ten children, dozens of grown-ups, and they still came for you. The countryside was a nightmare. In towns they were on leashes. They strained their ugly muzzles, wet and cold and those dumb holes for nostrils sniff sniff, but if you moved far enough away, hid behind your mother's skirts, there would a point at which you'd be out of reach, when the master or mistress, feeling too much pull on their arms would pull back, say 'sit'. They'd go on talking. They were all liars. They loved their dogs really, they loved their being out of control, they didn't care about you. You could feel it, how restrained their anger at the dog, how indulgent. Still. There was the leash. You watched the beast with wary glee, like the zoo animals behind their bars, the tiger going up and down, up and down. There was something absolute about the tiger. Fire. That would have been it, out of the cage, one bound, it. Almost better than the fear, with dogs it was nameless, you had to put up with it, a whole lifetime of putting up with it. The fear in the pit of your stomach. 'Be brave.' Sickening, it made her feel sick, the need to be brave. The worst form of needing to be good. At least to be good-good, all you had to do was sit quiet, like at table, or that concert her father had taken her to, he'd said, 'no noise at all, you mustn't cough, you mustn't sneeze, you mustn't fidget.' A catastrophe otherwise, he'd intimated. Everything destroyed if she made a noise. Rows and rows of people, all quiet, all these musicians in black. It had been agony. She'd choked the cough, the sneezes, her body had swallowed up the fidgets like turtles swallow their own limbs. She'd been heroic: she'd been good. She was a good daughter. She was good at school too. Except sometimes the devil got hold of her, shook her up, and things came out, words she didn't know she knew . . . But mostly not, mostly she was good, so good. With her little brother, it was an advantage being the oldest, with him also, she was good. Covered him up if he lost his blankets, did not rub the thin hair where on top of the skull a pulse beat. You could have pushed . . . No, she did not. But that need to be brave-good. She could not. That was the one she could not control. Terror shook her up, it was like the fireworks, one spark in the pit of her belly and it exploded into her limbs, her mouth. She shook she screamed. She threw herself on the ground she yelled. She stamped her feet, her cheeks were bathed in tears, snot dribbling from her nose into her mouth. The terror the terror. It was the only thing. Adults took note, in the end oh god in the end they removed the dog. She did not care. Did not care a bit. The nods of disapproval. The owners' wounded look. As long as they, the beasts, were behind a door.

Grown-ups didn't understand. It was surprising, they had been children after all. Perhaps by becoming grown-up you changed so completely there was nothing left, you became somebody else. Yes, that was the thing, by becoming a grown-up you changed your nature. You no longer sinned for a start, you were good without having to try, you were right all the time. That must be agreeable. Something to look forward to.

That was where you broke down. Anna didn't know, yet she knew. You broke down because something in you knew that you were right about dogs, you knew things about dogs the grown-ups didn't know, laughed about: but there was no way you could explain, nothing you could say to make them see. And you were ashamed. Terrible to be right and in mortal terror and also wrong because you knew you shouldn't have been. Oh the screams, the tramping of the ground, the one thing that made people take note.

Hysterical, the grown-ups said. The child's hysterical. They looked worried. That was enjoyable. Being hysterical was enjoyable too. You let go. Something stronger and dark and delightful because all you had to do was let it be, shake you up. The surrender. A wave catching you, powerless, it owned you. Not being hysterical: that was hard.

They did not know. How the dogs sniffed. How underhand they were. Blackie, in the lobby of the hotel. Her mother at the desk, talking to the owner. Two dogs, there were two dogs. A yellow one, Dick: a bad one, so they kept him behind doors. Anna could hear him scratching, the rumbling throat, the thunder of the barks. The shadow of the head behind the plated glass. Private it said: the office, the owner's quarters. Blackie is nice they said. No need to lock Blackie up. Look, he doesn't even bark. There, (they took her hand, they made it touch the matted black fur), nice doggie. Nice. She withdrew her hand as soon as they let go of her wrists. She got hold of her mother's leg, through the skirt. The skirt had little white patterns on black, pretty pattern. 'Really this is too much,' her mother said. 'Now Anna this is enough, at least let me sign the register in peace.' Anna had moved away. Blackie was sniffing her. It pushed its muzzle under her skirt. She kept pushing it away, but she didn't dare push too hard: he might bite. Blackie was against her pants. It was hot, it was wet, it was funny-cold. It started nibbling her, pushing right between her legs. It was . . . a wave . . . was it . . . pleasant? Oh no, that's not allowed. God, no. Saint Christopher make him go away. She stood, paralysed: Saint Christopher did nothing. And she could not tell Mummy. She didn't know why. She just knew.

Even so, Blackie was not so bad. As long as you stayed

glued to a grown-up, or climbed onto something. But Dick. The yellow one. It was a lie that they didn't let him out. He managed to get out. They thought it was funny. Oh yes she knew: the grown-ups were not reliable. They did not care. They pretended they could control the world. Anna believed them. But then there was no recourse: when they did not.

Like the time Dick somehow was out. Anna was by the roadside, she saw him. A blond cannon-ball, shooting out as the motor-bike swept past the curve. A man and a woman on it. Dick after them. Anna screaming. She didn't remember what had followed, but now there were the man and the woman. Covered in dust. Blood on their hands. They had crashed. Lucky they weren't hurt. They were white under the dust. Anna knew the colour of fear-white. It was imprinted in the pit of her stomach. They were telling the owner off. Mrs Fawcett kept saying how sorry she was, was there anything she could do. She was lying. Anna knew: if she really wanted to do something she would never, ever, let Dick out, or she would kill him, yes. The couple were shy. They did not dare protest too much. The man had turned up one of his trouser legs, there were the marks of the bite on his shin, red holes from which the blood seeped. There was white foam around them, where Mrs Fawcett had disinfected with hydrogen peroxide. 'We'll be all right,' the man kept saying. Mrs Fawcett had given them brandy. 'You shouldn't keep a dog like that, he might kill somebody,' the man said. He had a moustache. He was too kind. Anna wanted him to scream and rave, god why didn't he tell her, 'I'll go to the police, destroy this dog, you terrible woman.' But no, he was shy, he was polite. You could see he was poor. The clothes. The shyness. How relieved he was the motorbike was not ruined. He was grateful for the attention, the hydrogen peroxide, the drink. He was intimidated by these people from the hotel. The woman with him sat and shook. She had her arms round his waist, on the motorbike. Her jacket was covered in dust. The handlebars had been twisted, Mr Fawcett twisted them back into shape. The man was grateful. Anna shook with passionate indignation.

And so when the older children played the trick on her. In the downstairs room where they played games they told her she was safe, Dick was nowhere around, and she started relaxing and playing — and then someone opened the door, and Dick bounded. The yellow thing with fangs bounded. No faster than Anna, she was perched on the ping-pong table even before she screamed. Safe: Blackie would not have followed. But Dick was young. The big children were urging him on: Jump, Dick, jump.

He jumped. They were all laughing. Sunshine outside.

Anna screamed.

She could remember he had not bitten her. If anything, he had seemed puzzled. 'Not a bad dog,' the big children had said. 'He's young. He just likes to chase motorbikes. Wouldn't hurt a fly really.'

How could they, Anna thought. The powerlessness: being a child. Nobody believed you. Nobody did what you told them. They all thought Dick was nice. They took him out on walks.

And that time in the clearing.

Earlier they'd found lilies-of-the-valley, at the foot of a dark tree. Moss, shade. The miracle of these flowers. The green leaves unfurling, the tiny buds a sculptured white. Then the barking. Anna knew. She had spent the walk keeping out of Dick's way, close to one or other of the grown-ups: not for a minute had she forgotten about him. Except for that one minute when she'd crouched down by the flowers, her head between her knees and the skirt dangling between, while she looked and stuck her nose close to the corollas. She shouldn't have. Her attention should never have relented. It was as if the intensity of her watchfulness alone had controlled the thing, and now it was loose, barking, and she knew what it meant: evil.

She'd run ahead into the clearing. A meadow. In the middle, a white goat, tethered by a chain to a post. Next to her, a kid. Fragile. Adorable. Dick was trying to kill the kid, and the goat was fighting to save it. Dick kept growling, circling, jumping. The goat plunged towards him, her horns forward. Impeded by her chain. The kid, bewildered, terrified, seeking refuge between the mother's legs, hampered her charge even more. 'Oh hurry, hurry,' Anna was screaming. 'Save the goat, oh save the kid.'

The adults weren't even running. They were taking stock. They were watching. 'Oh hurry hurry,' Anna screamed and cried and pulled them by the hand and pushed them from behind. And still they did not run. Anna knew, so how could they not? It was like Monsieur Seguin's little white goat. She wanders up the mountain and in the evening she meets the wolf. She fights bravely, her little horns forward, till her strength is exhausted. At night the wolf kills her. Dick was the wolf. Anna had known all along. Anna could see. Dick had bitten one of the goat's teats. It was torn, it was bleeding. The goat couldn't swerve fast enough, the collar round her neck strangling her as she charged, the chain jolting her back. It was so disgusting, the mother tethered, she couldn't even fight properly. Oh hurry hurry, the powerlessness the powerlessness, and the rage. All black. The scream. That would make them take note. The scream would rein in that wolf of a dog.

Anna could not remember what had happened then, except that in the end the goat and kid had been saved. She'd never forgotten the bleeding teat, the kid unsteady on its legs, in the way of its mother's hooves. Nor the rush of the great yellow body, which the adults thought was nice. 'He's only young.'

He'd come in, he'd been so kind. There was such light in his eyes. Green. Like the day when she'd been about to tell him it was no good, they shouldn't see each other any more, and the clarity of his eyes, that could be so black, his eyes gold-green in the sun, with flecks of grey, had so moved her. That she hadn't been able to say it.

And there they were.

'You'll have to be very courageous my love,' he'd said.

'My brother,' she'd said. She'd breathed deeply. She'd known, straight away.

'Is there no hope?' she'd asked, and then she hadn't even waited for the answer. She'd been ashamed she'd asked. That wasn't being brave. She'd better learn.

And she had learned, boy, hadn't she learned. She had grown. Somehow, without being aware of it, she had ceased throwing fits. There was the crying, yes. At twelve, nothing if not dramatic, she would burst into tears at the dinner table, rush into her bedroom. Sob against the bed. Her father followed. He would sit on the bed, and talk. How she loved him for it. There were these sources of love, so deep, beyond memory.

Anna and her mother. Together. Alone. Anna was in a cot. She could remember that the top of her arms only reached the top of the bars. But she could walk. Stand up. Above, there were no bars.

Her mother had said something. About somebody coming. It was the war. Anna did not know. Things were dark.

Perhaps it was only the light. And the door had opened. Anna had jumped to her feet. She had screamed, 'Papa!' In her family they did not say 'daddy'. Her mother had not said who it was. But Anna had guessed. Had known.

Springing to her feet. Screaming 'Papa!'. Being caught up in the man's arms. Lifted up.

The dark room. The cot. Standing up like the bars.

And why then all her life, the fear of men? The tormented belly? Why then in her childhood the fear of dogs?

She had learned. Only at times the bursting into tears, Only when alone, in woods, screaming to the trees, or by the edge of seas, the waves. Locked up in the toilet, at school, during the breaks, the lunch hours. Her mother so ill, away. Her mother's body, wracked with migraines, and now, when there was a death, someone close to her, the terrible diarrhoeas.

How Anna's mother had rushed home from her son's, Will's, funeral. She had left Anna and the other mourners staring down the rectangle of the hole. Rushed down the path to the waiting funeral cars. Anna running after her. The mother through clenched teeth: 'Go back. Leave me alone.' Later in bed, white.

So confusing, these intertwined deaths. Boundaries had become porous. Things circulated. Too much. And again. You could not stop them. Anna's mother had lost a son, Will. Who was Anna's brother. One year before, to the day, Anna's mother had lost her own brother, Angus. Anna had been with her. Now, almost a year later, almost day for day, Anna feared for her son. He was leaving her. Returning to England, to his father. He was only catching a plane. She would see him again. And the churning in your belly, irrational, so foolish, Anna. History never repeats itself.

Bodies are separate.

Ah but what if you've been inside, are still inside? What if your own son Paul is still inside, in some terrible way, and you have to leave the dark bubble of this air terminal, let him go let him go and you yourself go forth into the streaming American twilight, look for Route 2 and the cabin in the woods?

Belly churning.

Like her mother's. After Angus's death. He'd always been the mysterious distant glamorous relative, this one brother of her mother's, Anna's only uncle. He had moved in a more elevated sphere, he partied with people they only read about in the papers.

Anna had been in London with her mother, in Angus's thickly carpeted, thickly brocaded apartment. Sorting out Angus's things. It felt like a violation, things so refined, so sweetly guarded and ordered. So . . . male. Anna had been so entranced by him the few times he'd taken her out: the exquisite pin-striped suits, the leather smell of the car interior, tea at Brown's, your head swimming from the thrill, the folds of the wool cloth, the body stretching the cloth. The gold-tipped Sobranie cigarettes. How you worshipped handsome men if you were a plain woman. The uncle had dined at Claridge's, he took fashion models out. Now he was dead. A heart attack. He had been alone. That very night he had made a will. 'I bequeath to my beloved sister . . .' They'd found it next to his head, on his desk.

They'd been sorting his things, Anna and her mother. In the elegant, strangely muffled apartment. Half-shade from the thick brocade curtains. The heady scent of flowers from the funeral. A woman friend of the uncle's had visited, a lover perhaps. She regarded them, it was clear, Anna and her mother, as interlopers: vultures who'd descended on Angus's furniture, just because they were family, when they had seen so little of him during his life. Why had he bequeathed all his worldly goods to his sister, I ask you? The woman friend wore a mink coat made of a thousand tiny bits of fur. Her whole body had that air of polish, each bit, skin, eyes, cheeks, mouth, lips, hair, processed and painted and scented and glossy: a real woman. She had come to buy what she thought Angus should have bequeathed, or given, to her. A diamond bracelet. There they were, the woman, Anna, and her mother, each of them aware of what the others were thinking, being polite, each grieving in her own way, on the dead uncle's Regency chairs. And suddenly Anna's mother had rushed out of the room. 'Is your mother ill?' the woman had said; 'yes,' Anna had answered, not wanting to follow her mother, not to embarrass her further. Give her time to wash. Anna making conversation oh, she had learned, she could pretend to be calm, nobody like herself to be good-good, trust Anna to look dignified, put a brave face on it. Anna hating the woman because she too had smelt the smell, she knew, did she think: 'There is grief here after all', did it occur to her, sister, mother, whatever the gaps in space, in time . . .? Or did she think: 'Serves her right. Greedy vulgar bitches'?

Anna's mother leaning over the jade basin, washing her pants under Angus's swan's neck brass taps. Refusing help. 'Get out of here.' The smell. Refusing the refuge of Anna's arms. Holding herself together. Refusing to cry.

Her mother good-good. Brave-brave mother.

She'd drunk the broth Anna had made, though.

The smell. Oh how Anna hated her own belly. The endless betrayal. Croaking of frogs, hissing of snakes. The sick headaches, the sour smell, which her husband hated. Stomach knotted, no food can pass my lips. Stomach swelling, and the four winds raging from the four corners of the horizon. When you were children you could laugh, like Will and his little friends who had a farting competition under the grandmother's windows and the grandmother had leant out and shouted, 'Careful, children, the motorbike's coming out the garage!' How they had laughed and laughed rolling in the grass, by the brook, till their eyes were streaming. Why could you do it when you were children, when you also knew about dogs, when your brother and his little friends tormented you with your fear of dogs, they weren't frightened, swinging the basket they'd been sent to fill with raspberries from Mrs Stone's garden, and Anna knew that as soon as they'd opened and closed the gate, begun the climb to the old lady's orchard, a wild bevy of dogs would rush all over them, barking, jumping. Will teased: but he was there, smaller than herself, his head level with the dogs' jaws, laughing into their faces, his hands all over their wet fangs, their fur. They licked his face. He laughed. Patronizing. No protection, no. But comfort, yes. The laughter. Level with it. Equal to the lords of fear. Meet for the world. And she was with him. The golden curls. The little hands, so firm, so quick that grabbed the fur, and stroked. The lovely way he had of opening his hands as if to say, 'How can you expect me to know?' The long lashes, that Anna so envied. The shadows on his cheeks.

Meet for the world. So much more so than she was.

'Spastic colon,' the doctor said. 'Cause unknown. Very frequent. No cure. Sensible diet. Try to avoid stress.'

She had taken the enemas. She'd done it in the discreetest way, creeping to the bathroom at six in the morning, then two hours later. Let nobody suspect. And even so. Even so, after the tube had been inserted, after half-naked Anna had lain absurdly prostrate on her side and the vaselined pipe had been inserted, and air had been blown into her, a bellyful of air, winds from the four corners, till it hurt, and she thought, chinese torture, disembowelment: as the air had come out it had brought out with it a disgusting yellowish scum. It had gone through the tube into a bottle. There it was, in a glass jar, absurd disgusting, like froth on top of a beer mug. The doctor and his assistant saddled with it. Anna wanted to apologize, apologize for what? Having a body that produced . . . but Anna, everybody else's did. Oh no. Now that that they were no longer children, now that they had learnt, that they were grown up, that you had to control, to hide, deny, there was no excuse for having a belly that produced such stuff. 'Spastic colon,' the doctor said. He had a moustache. She tried not to look him in the eyes. He had seen her arse. Her cunt. Not that they were so bad, Anna thought sometimes. The folds of pink. The shapely hips, round and white like her mother's, which she had seen, that time, when her mother was washing her pants half-naked at the sink. What beautiful hips my mother's got, Anna had thought. The hidden beauty of those hips that nobody, not even her father, ever saw: her parents had ceased sleeping together when Anna was a child. Mother so ill after brother's birth. Could not have another. Mother a devout Catholic.

Anna was trying not to look at the doctor. She'd liked the feel of his hands. She was not supposed to like the feel of his hands. It was medicine. You were supposed to feel nothing. The disaster would be complete if on top of being seen by the doctor to be so disgusting she were to start desiring him. Spastic colon. Only abnormal people like myself, Anna had thought, could start desiring a man who'd seen them in their abjection.

Perverse. That's what her husband said she was. What

her books were.

And so she'd gone through this shame, she had subjected the doctor to this disgusting stuff, all for nothing. Well, it was nice to know it was nothing. She'd thought, ulcer, or worse. But no, it was nerves.

A hysteric when you were a child, Anna thought.

Driving. She'd noted nothing, not the queues at the airport nor the traffic out, the dusk turning to night. Only the rain, the random steady water scythed into ever-collapsing sheaves by the windscreen wipers. Blurred world peopled by white, yellow, red lights, wet world outside. The car a dry bubble, darkness besieged by water, and Anna at the wheel.

Oh but she'd grown over the years, she'd grown and learnt. There seemed to be no end to the learning. Be brave. Pick up the telephone when you'd rather throw yourself out of the window. And she picked it up. Go in and interview these women in jail, when everything, the smells, the walls, the endless sound of keys, the bars, all that clinking metal, froze her. 'Anna is weird,' people would say. 'I wonder what kicks she gets out of writing about women murderers. Something in her childhood perhaps? I pity her husband.'

She could not say, 'In my childhood I was afraid of dogs. I am trying to face my fear. I have to do it by extremes cause it's easier for me to leap in with both feet than just walk up to it.' She couldn't say, 'I am less afraid of tigers than of dogs.' And yet even leaping in did not help. Even going into the cage. It, whatever it was, occurred somewhere else. Bellies were deep as the ocean. You touched some levels, the waves flung themselves, the wind tossed them. You thought you knew pity, you knew indignation, you faced up to terror. But you'd got nowhere. What you brought from the depths was just froth. Wind and froth. There was no end to sea-diving. The more you coped, the more you learned, the less you knew.

And Belly raged. Oh raged.

She had tried so hard, after her brother's death. Fill up the gap. Let us, through love, keep him alive. Be of comfort to each other. It all went to show, didn't it? How little she knew. About grief, as about everything else. How grief tore at people. It had been palpable, this August when they'd gone to Bristol, the parents' place, close to the sea. The cliffs. The close-cropped grass. Somewhere, on the other side of town, the cemetery. Anna's brother Will had chosen to be buried away from the family plot. The childhood church. He had gone as far away from his parents as he could, while still remaining in town. From his bedroom window, in the terraced house at the top of the hill, one could see the blue hills and the edge of the wood where the parents' house nested.

What a cry there had been in this choosing to be so near. What a refusal in his will: that he should be buried away from them all. All by himself.

The thinness. The pain. The courage. And oh, the pain. He would rage at times, between clenched teeth. Hollow eyes. You could not press him in your arms, there was such agony in his chest. Everything had packed up, in bits and pieces. He'd suffered the agony alone. Concealed it from them all. When she'd found out, it was almost the end. When she came to see him, he was beyond morphine even, which made him sick. He could only see her a little. He would not see the parents at all. They kept phoning, sending messages. 'What can I do?' Anna's father had asked. 'I can't tell him that I love him, can I?' 'Of course you can,' Anna had cried. 'That is exactly what you must do.' The father had tried. It had made no difference. It was only in novels that a parent, a child said, 'I love you,' and the son or the father cried and had what they had wanted all along and all was forgiven. Anna's brother had not forgiven.

'I never feel at ease with the parents,' Will had said. 'Never have. They never cared for me. Never gave me what I wanted. If my father had been able to love me, I wouldn't have needed to seek love from other men. I wouldn't be dying of this shit now.'

'They're both tyrannical and cold,' Will had said. 'Now they say they want to see me!'

'But they love you,' Anna had said. 'They're clumsy. They're messed up. They're repressed. They don't know how to show it.'

'They're unable to feel anything for anybody else but themselves,' he'd said. 'I don't want to see them.'

Anna's eyes turned to the window. Between some trees, now bared by winter, you could make out the slate grey of a roof. The roof of the parents' house.

How tyrannical their father could be. He thought he was being fatherly. He thought he was providing fatherly authority. He could not bear to have his will opposed. His world was threatened with chaos if things did not go exactly his own way, if his order was in the least shaken.

He gave his son no space. He and Will would drive each other to paroxysms of rage and grief, and the father would assert his power. 'This is my house. Your brother doesn't understand me. How can I have a dancer for a son? And the company he keeps. He does everything he can to provoke me. Do you know what? On his last visit home he actually broke a wall. Brought down the partition between the two little bedrooms. His lordship wanted a bigger bedroom. This is my house. He didn't even ask for permission. Just took a mallet and hammered down the wall.'

Unmendable breaches. Will was howling, his dancer friend James close to him, silent, with his gentle brown eyes, pleading for support. 'I can't stand this any more,' the brother was howling. 'My father never does anything for me. He never lets me do anything.'

How can you explain to a father why his son demolishes partitions in his house? You can't: the father just feels aggrieved. Aggressed. Drapes himself in his hurt, his dignity. 'Don't talk nonsense, Anna. This is simply outrageous.'

You could know something about both sides. You could know that people somewhere loved each other. You could not tell them. You could not explain. You were powerless. Your heart could break for grief at your brother's pain, and you could do nothing for him. Not even share it. You felt pain in your chest. Your belly. You felt pain at your arms that could not even press the thin torso to your chest, because of the extremity of the pain in it. You had arms and a belly and knees that had embraced, supported, held the baby that your brother had been. You had held him in your arms, you remembered oh so vividly, the blond curls, the long lashes. On all fours he challenged, he defied the father. Who got mad. On all fours at full speed he pursued the mother. Did she push him away? 'Child, pull yourself together.' If so, how come she, Anna, had not known, had not opened her arms, held him tight? How come she hadn't given him what he felt had been so denied him? She had not understood. She had not known. So absorbed in herself.

The silence in the brother's bedroom. The net curtains, long, so white they seemed blue, so still. Hiding the window through which ... The brother slept. Anna had almost forced his door. Sleep, sleep, my beloved. Perhaps when you sleep you do not feel the pain. It was a sleep more like swooning. From the extremity of the pain. He had been so beautiful. His grace. His bounding. Anna's pride, seeing him on stage. So venturesome, her little brother. He could fly. Such wonderful friends. Meet for the world, my little brother. A match for the dogs.

The hounds of death had got him.

Will did not want to be seen in his thinness. He did not want them to watch him suffer. Perhaps he did not want her at all, either. Perhaps he also thought, if she'd loved me enough . . . The tenderness that had never been met. The cry that had not found an ear.

'Papa! Papa! lift me up!'

Perhaps she'd had it all. She had demanded it all. The fear, the fits: blackmail? So that the little brother should not get it from her? Who knew, oh God, who knew? Except that he was dead, the little brother. That he had suffered the unspeakable agonies alone. They, the father, the mother, Anna, with her own beautiful son Paul, who was so like Will, had followed the funeral. Dignified. One mustn't show one's grief. Be brave. 'The thing you've got to understand, Anna,' Will had said, 'is how alone you are when you die.'

Powerless, silent, love had howled.

And now Will lay alone, on the other side of the Atlantic. Anna's husband and Anna had come home from America in the summer for a visit to the parents in their Bristol house. Mend fences, Anna had thought. Comfort each other. Fill the gap. She'd had to fly back to her American job, to Paul who'd wanted an American summer, had stayed in the cabin in the woods, playing the woodcutter like his father before him.

She'd no sooner gone than the row had erupted.

She'd no sooner gone from her parents', leaving her husband with them, counting on her husband to care for them, keep them company a few more days, than her father had played up. The old tyrant had reappeared. He'd lent his darling old Mercedes to his son-in-law . . . Now he found that the oil, the water levels had not been properly checked. They were dangerously low. He had found it out at the end of a pub crawl on which his son-in-law had taken him. Out of kindness. To distract him.

'Can I have the keys to the car back, please?' the father had said.

The husband had no car there. And no money. His parents-in-law were keeping him. He was waiting for Anna to send money. When she got her next pay cheque.

He'd gone out of his mind with rage.

He'd telephoned Anna. Screamed at her. Called her father all the names under the sun. 'Impossible old man. Senile. Bloody bastard.' 'I'll show him,' he'd said. He'd hung up on Anna. 'You stupid bitch,' he'd said. As Anna tried to pacify him, to say, 'He'll calm down, he's just old, too much grief, doesn't know what he's doing.' Anna had been having this lovely peaceful time with Paul. Mother and son, out to spoil each other. She was feeding him huge breakfasts of pancakes. He was making her a woodpile.

She'd phoned home. Her mother had been in tears. 'Your husband made a dreadful scene,' she'd said. 'He came and threatened us. Called your father all the names under the sun. Said he was fed up with you, all things were at an end between the two of you. He was drunk. He was terrifying. Your father was shaking. Your husband said that he would forbid Paul ever to see us again. And now we're terrified that you too will hate us.' The mother's voice. So frail on the telephone. So charged with sorrow it vibrated, shrank to a hushed whisper. 'As soon as your mother's alone she cries,' her father had said. 'It'll blow over,' Anna had said. 'Everybody's upset.' 'Not this time, Anna,' her mother had replied. 'Too much has happened. We're too old.' Her mother had been ill. In bed. One of her diarrhoeas . . .

Anna's impotent rage. Yes, my father's impossible, but my husband? Two old people who've just lost their son, and he couldn't restrain himself . . . Who knows but that he too had been raging against the bars, the keys withdrawn from him, the claustrophobia . . . Tiger, tiger . . .

'Don't you believe a word the old liar says to you,' her husband had screamed on the telephone. 'All he does is lie.'

The man enters the darkened bedroom. Your body springs, it knows, the exquisiteness, the tenderness of the man who's just entered the room. The arms raised, the body lifted up above, out of, the bars. 'Papa!'

The man had not entered. He had not materialized. He had not held out his arms. And her brother, who had raged and broken bars and partitions, had not been lifted up into anyone's arms.

She could never, never undo it.

Will. The black lips. 'How alone you are when you die.'

She could never, never stop loving the man. Knowing what tenderness there could be in the arms. The eyes.

Belly raged.

There had been Paul. Cutting wood for her. Like his father the year before in that same cabin in the woods, when he'd come in with the green-gold light in his eyes and said, 'you're going to have to be very courageous, my love.'

She could not hate him either.

Paul now. Cutting wood for her. So that she would be warm in winter. Every time she lit a fire, every log she brought up from the basement to lay in the hearth, she'd think of her son.

Now he was leaving. She'd driven him to the airport. He was going to join his father. God knew for what future. She'd said goodbye to him. Now she was driving back to the house in the woods. Where he would no longer be.

I am telling you straight. I know about Anna. I know Anna inside out. I am a cry issuing from her belly. It will reach to the ends of the earth.

I do not know about any of the people whose names appear here in relation to Anna. Father mother maternal uncle husband brother son, we might have a lover also, why not? Who knows whether they exist, whether they are in Anna's memory, part of the pageant of passion that feeds her cry? Perhaps Anna has dreamt them up, to give her grief a shape. Of one thing I am certain: she does not mimic them, she does not act them out. Things are much too urgent for pretence. When the heart is large as a moon, heavy as a cannon ball, when it drops to the bottom of the belly that is deep as a deep-water well and yet has no bottom, there is no space there is no time for make-believe. No stage here, no audience. A reader maybe, whose heart should be growing like a moon.

Anna cannot afford to think. If she thought, she would see him. His blond hair. Her son is beautiful as a god, his blond hair falls on his forehead. He has a shy laugh, his legs are comely. Her brother is beautiful like an angel, he bounds on-stage, a dolphin of the air. His blond hair curls close on his head, waved back. His eyelashes are so long they make a shadow on his cheeks.

They made a shadow even when he was dead. They pulled the drawer open, as in a filing-cabinet. He had a number on. He was pale as the moon, he was lean as death. His blond hair curled, neatly waved back. They had put ointment on his skin, to preserve him, she supposed. When she kissed his forehead she had a taste of poison on her lips. All day.

The belly churns. Death churns in the belly. From the belly it will begin to explode. The grave in which they put him they sealed with a stone like the filing-cabinet drawer. With the cement it fitted the hole neatly.

No more breaking of partitions, little brother.

She drove into the night. She saw him: her son whom she'd just left, who was going to cross the ocean. Standing in front of the airport, the only one she saw amid the jostle. His head inclined gracefully to one side, waving. He is shy, it was not a large gesture, just a hand raised, and she knew he too wanted to cry. Dark, with the light from the brilliant interior shining through the glass doors on to his golden hair. He was standing there. He had to leave. To make his life.

She was lucky. He was alive, he was young. She was alive. She had a wood house to go to, a bed in which to sleep. He would go on living. Oh yes he would.

Her mother had raised her eyes. They were driving past her brother's windows, they were in a taxi. Anna's belly had tightened as they were approaching, a hard knot, keep yourself together, don't show that you recognize the street. The street with a house with a flat behind the windows of which your brother is dying.

Don't let your mother see that you recognize the street, that you are thinking about your brother. 'The worst of it is, I keep thinking it's a nightmare, I keep thinking I'm going to wake up and it won't be true,' the mother had said. They were waiting, at the dentist's. Perhaps your mother's mind has drifted away, perhaps she is asleep somewhere, and she won't recognize . . .

Her mother turned her head. She raised her eyes to the windows. She looked. She did not look sad. She did not sob. She did not even sigh.

She was calling and he did not hear.

That turn of the head. Those eyes raised to the windows. There were lights shining behind the curtains.

Oh mother goat your kid is dead.

Anna is lucky. Her son is alive. She will miss him, but so what? She must be brave. Driving into the night, alone, because now he has left. Alone in the vastness of America, five thousand miles before she could hit the Pacific, her back to the Atlantic, for she was heading due West. 2 West, it said. Obscurely, she wished it had been 3.

His hands on the wheel. Alternately absent-minded and decisive, competing with other drivers. Playful as a child.

The beauty of his shoulders.

Dancing brother.

Men's bodies. The beauty of men's bodies. Your lips on a shoulder.

Several times she thought she'd got lost. Then she thought she had a flat tyre. Bloomedoon doon doon the tyres went. Is it the road, is it the tyres? In Italy, ages ago, they'd been travelling with her father. The driver was one of her father's assistants, Michael, a handsome young doctor, six foot or so, hair black as jet. Dark glasses like a gangster, gentle as a lamb. At the wheel, oozing the most exquisite respect for his boss. Bloomedoon doon doon the tyres had gone. Did you hear that noise, Michael? her father had asked. You've got a flat tyre. They'd stopped. The wheels looked all right. Drove on again. Bloomedoon doon doon, the tyres had sung. I assure you, Michael, what you are doing is highly dangerous, her father had said. You must change that tyre. In the end poor Michael had changed the tyre that looked the least solid, by the light of a streetlamp. Bloomedoon doon doon. Anna's father had almost made Michael stop and look for a garage, another tyre. Then the noise, magically, had stopped: dents in the road. The father had laughed. Michael had not even let out a squeak of protest. What a sweet temper. He was with his boss.

One did not oppose the boss. You never opposed the boss. The world went better if you did not. You weren't even critical.

The world was full of bosses.

The brother's hands in the jaws of the dogs, pushing: laughing.

'Anna, I wish you'd keep your perversity for your writing,' this man had said, the man she couldn't stop wanting to make love to. She'd met him on a train. He was a Bulgarian, he was called Sasha. So youthful-looking despite his white hair. Almost boyish. She'd begun to dream about him. He was so gentle in her dream. Kissing her eyes, her cheeks, her chin. He was slender, in the bed he held her close and oh so gently. You were not the master of your dreams, or should you say mistress? They were supposed to tell you what you really felt, to put you in touch with your deeper self. In a dream she had met her parents, her father held his mother by the arm, as he always did, and they both stood tall as they always did. Frail now. Frail. They were wandering, they were looking for their son. They'd lost him. He'll get better, she'd said, he's tough, he'll survive. But she could not comfort them. It was dark it was night something was green, a café perhaps and she kept meeting them, she too was looking for the lost son. Well, that other dream in which Sasha was making love to her, what was it telling her? Nothing that helped, either. That she wished for a man to make gentle love to her? She knew. Only, it was harder having it almost happen in the luminous dark of the dream. Your dreams moulded people to what you wished they were. They also made you into the person you longed to be, someone who would find it easy to go to bed with a man, when something in you spoke, something called, something even more submerged than the bottom of the well. Less so. Yes, less so. That something had a voice, a voice that at times could be triumphant. That something could sing, it could cry. It could issue this dull, this ignorant, this dumb appeal. Dumb, for you did not know whether the man had the same voice in him: probably not. If you let on, if you let it show, you'd be covered with ridicule. Dumb as that voice was, though, it thudded, it throbbed, it flared up, it flooded you at times with shocking images, oh no I could not, not that. Unacceptable. You'd repressed the voice: but you'd heard. That other thing though, where the fear was, where death was, that other thing that fed it all and messed it all up, that other thing couldn't get itself heard.

'Anna, I wish you'd save your perversity for your books, and kept it out of your life.' That was what Sasha had said. You'd been teasing him about politics. That was what he thought of you. Your books. Your talk. That man you couldn't stop yourself desiring. He probably wasn't even any good at love. How could he be? His two wives had divorced him.

One after the other. Oh Anna: sour grapes. He had no patience with views that questioned his. Her views. He was supposed to be wise: an atheist, a social realist, a philosopher. He said she was perverse. She hadn't replied. She'd taken it. She could take anything. She was: perverse. He hadn't meant it that way. But that way too.

Her mother could have gone to see her brother. Surely, even at this late stage, when he was closing his door on them all, when he was saving his strength to meet the suffering, surely she could still have gone, she could have said, I love you. Surely she could? Surely there must be a way of letting people know, of . . .

Anna and her son were shy of each other. It was as if the great yearning, the great love, had to be shown in little ways, some pancakes she'd make, a t-shirt she'd buy him when she was short of cash, her listening to views she did not share, telling him that he would be all right, he had so much to give. She looked at him: she worshipped him. She had never seen such beauty in a man. She had seen that beauty in her brother. She took photographs of him in his red shirt, wielding an axe, making her a wood pile: his way of loving her. His wood would remain, was stacked high in the basement . . .

There had been a frightful storm. Torrents of rain, red and gold leaves driving in whirls against the windscreen. She'd had to drive the last few miles ever so slowly. She had not changed the tyres. Nobody to tell her what to do. There was an advantage to being alone.

The house was in total darkness.

The hill leading up to the house was in total darkness.

The heavy car stopped. Anna switched off the lights. Got out. Rain, wind, darkness. Leaves raining down, which you felt, heard, peopling the woods with their falling. One brushed

Anna's cheek. Vegetal, cool. Wet.

Inside was peopled with the son's presence. Paul's body was everywhere. The couch on which he had lain, booted ankles crossed, tossing back his hair, face lengthening as he reflected before speaking. Red tartan shirt. His hand on the fridge. Drinking from the tap, leaning over the sink. His bed. He'd folded the sheets.

Honey-coloured house. The rain pattered like fingers on the wooden roof.

Anna grabbed the sheets. Held them tight.

He was going to be fine. Partings were difficult. He would be perfectly fine. Young people had to get away from their parents. Absence: that was all.

The house was vibrant with it. Not a bit of space where his body was not. Sitting at the table. Lacing up his boots on the stairs, before he went out to cut wood.

Anna fell to her knees.

She did not know how it happened.

There was this scream.

She had not screamed like this since she'd been a child. Was it her? She did not know. She heard it. It filled the space. Rocking to and fro, grabbing the sheets, on her knees.

It came from the depths of Anna's belly, the loud lament that filled the room, her son's room, the stairs, the golden downstairs room. Went through the walls, to meet the lashing rain, the downpour of leaves, gold, red. Went through the woods, the roads drowned in leaves and water, Route 2 that went back to the Atlantic, on the shore of which the son still was, ready to cross. It went over the Atlantic, the waves tossed on the shore, black under the no-moon sky, wet sky meeting the wet deep. It travelled over the Atlantic, faster than the ships, the planes, the wind, over and over up and down the winds, tossed and whirling and at times sucked up to the sky it went homeward, to the shore where the waves crashed, the cliffs where the waves roared and threw up their spume, and the house on the promenade where her mother did not cry but rocked silently, her belly twisted with grief, to the grave where her brother lay alone. Anna's cry wound its way into a crack in the stone, a split in the wood of the coffin. Wound itself round her brother's body, it crouched at his feet. It would mount guard.

From Anna's belly, from the depths that were before her, before she was, from the roots that reached deep into the organs, the depths of the organs, the caves of the underworld, from the fibres and along the rivers of the blood, the arteries where it pulsed like lava, the veins where it streamed, sluggish, ferrying its flotsam to the outer regions, Anna's scream travelled. It issued from her mouth, it had shape, a vapour, ectoplasm Anna thought, that's what it is. It rose and whirled and took shape, it had a body, elastic, it could contract and expand, flow into anything, it expanded now, like the smoke that released from the bottle which the fisherman has brought up from the depths of the sea, billows into a huge rising, substantial *Efrit*. Her insides were porous, the scream went through every partition, there were no bars, not any more. No boundaries outside, the scream went through the walls that were not walls but wood, through the woods and the rain that lashed and rocked it, sprinkled it with leaves, clothed it with a cloak of dead leaves, gold and brown and red, a wet mantle that the sea winds scattered. It travelled over the ocean, its substantial oh so material so containable body flying skidding over the waves, buffeted by the winds riding the winds, bounding. Playing. The dolphin scream went like thought over the waves, it bounded over the cliffs, it made its way to the cemetery, crept easily through the cement, into the grave. The screams were sounds were howls were words, oh how Anna screamed her brother's name, she oh how she screamed her son's name, and the grief for absence and the grief at death wound round each other like coils of smoke.

Out oh out. Nevermore. Nevermore oh belly nevermore the dogs turned back inside, devouring your entrails.

The names she screamed she howled.

It was good.

Anna knew she was screaming.

She was raging.

S. WHO LIVES OVER THE SIGN SHOP

Gail Scott

'What d'you call that thing?'
'A pe . . .'
'A pediment.'
'What's a pediment?'

The tall thin man with elegant clothes and long grey hair tucked behind his ears laughs and walks away.

The woman (still sitting in the bar) laughs too. With her air of someone from a Simone de Beauvoir novel, dressed in purple. Albeit, a slightly English accent when speaking French. A tense, almost voyeuristic tint to her gaze. Which now strays across the street again. Noting that the building has three storeys. Tacked to its top, where its stone façade meets its flat roof, is a high piece of ornamental metal flouncing painted burnt sienna. A fake pediment, really, because no depth. Running the building's width, with scrolled peak and the year 1904 written uncertainly in the middle, it leans slightly back upon the wide blue sky as if to brace itself against the weather. From there, a line of other flattopped roofs reaches down the street and curves around the corner under an azure ceiling with intermittent clouds. Reminiscent somehow of New Orleans.

The woman (V. for Violet, or possibly *la voyeuse*) looks down the building's front. Each storey, with its *quatour* of large square windows, seems to serve a different purpose. She gazes up once more to a large apartment window on the building's top floor. From the foliage in it, a plastic pink flamingo delicately sticks its neck out. Beneath, on the second floor, a sign shop. Its windows all blocked out with notices reading SIGNS/*ENSEIGNES* (*VENTE*, BARGAINS, *RABAIS*). The first floor's banal, commercial: a cheap clothing store with crooked awning. In a partly open door beside it stands a woman. V. gives a blink of recognition. Having seen that face somewhere.

A face that wanted love, that was certain. Sitting in some restaurant on The Main* with white skin and hennaed hair. Almost a travesty of self. Half flower. That withdrew. If you scratched it with a slightly-pointed nail. Half clown. Dragging her brightly-coloured vestments through the town. Hair purple-red. Painted forehead. Wrist protectors. Colour deflectors. Saggy leg-warmers. And the elusiveness of her gaze! An incredible clear colour of turquoise that melted away when you asked for information. The same eyes in all the faces of her various incarnations. Female junkie. Vogue model. Scorpio woman. Ageing punk. The physical beauty of each. And the secrets that went with them. How do you pay for your habit? someone asked her once. The answer: silence. The turquoise eyes reproachful before melting into absence. Briefly, as New Wave Artist, S. gave performances of astonishing black humour. Once, coming down the aisle in clown's colours, balancing pierrot-like on one foot with the other polka-dot leg sticking out in front, she pointed to

* The street that traditionally divided the minority English sector from the majority French-language sector in Montréal.

the leg and said, half sheepishly, half mocking:

'I think I have a hard-on.'

Now she comes out of the building across the street, dressed as a kind of mandarin. A pale version of her earlier self. In toned-down colours, hair less mauve than auburn, piled elegantly on her head. Make-up perfect, yet almost imperceptibly applied. Spotless light blouse and wide pants showing a certain oriental influence. Followed by a small Caucasian man with a pigtail down his back. They turn right and march along the sidewalk, her arm around his slender waist, towards the healthfood store. As if they lived a perfectly ordered life. Then back again, and through the bar door. Sitting at a table. Except, the restless male gets up and leaves quite quickly. She (currently a redhead) watching him. The pale line of her cheek, with the powder pretty well concealing a slight loosening of the skin, apparently untroubled by his action. As if the departure of a lover could only be incidental, so great the pain was elsewhere.

'How do you pay for your habit?' the acquaintance had persisted. Angry at the elusiveness in S.'s gaze. (*In the dream, S.'s walking away. A boarded up house. You're robbed. Her indifference [the junkie connection]. But it doesn't frighten you.*) Finally the acquaintance (V., to tell the truth), having heard rumours, said the ultimate to be vengeful: 'Feminism would help you ground yourself. Uh, help you stop living with guys who chase you with studded belts.' S's voice, almost expressionless:

'*Je te crois un peu ja-louse de mes amants.*'

V. watches patiently. Across the street, the door blows slightly open. Revealing only wooden stairs climbing to her flat. Some sign-shop men descend carrying a ladder. They march down the street, turn, march back again, the ladder held between them. They're carrying a sign. For a moment in the bar, in a space between songs on the radio, there is silence in which V. feels the anguish of suspension in the coming heat of summer. Especially without love. Or with it if one has fear of losing. '*Qu'il fait chaud*!' says the redhead across the room. Asking the waitress for orange juice.

V. glances at the window with the pink flamingo, now leaning back, slightly. Wondering, retrospectively, if it's the window of her bedroom. The dresser in it with, no doubt, rounded corners and stained dark, 50s style. On which sit all the pots that keep her beautiful. The small wooden stick to put on khol. The envelope of henna for her hair. Some jewellery. The room smelling vaguely of her perfume. Light shines across the floor and off the convex mirror. The window's closed, but you can hear the traffic in the street. The room may also carry, like many empty rooms, the echo of its owner's voice: its flatness. Carrying not a trace of its native French.

Oddly, on the phone, that same flat voice came through rich, erotic. As if the self were best projected through technology. A voice (before V. had actually met its owner in the flesh) magnetized by telephone wires. Conjuring up in the mind an image of white rooms, with low bed on which to stretch one's body. A kitchen with a beautiful earthy woman and fragrant coffee, dripping into a nice ceramic pot. The whole scene radiating with the sensuality of a house that's clean with drawers neatly ordered, scented, perhaps, with blossoms, windows gleaming, bedclothes fresh, unwrinkled. And the tray, when deposited (by the still-imagined S., a woman with ample breasts and flowing skirt) near the bed that V. was lolling on, would have a small vase of dried blue flowers on it.

Except in person, S. turned out to be a kind of emaciated drag queen. Appearing at a women's exhibition in the museum, all dressed in black. Lace gloves cut off knuckle-length. She lifted one such gloved hand and twirled her fingers in the curls of a woman standing there. Then disappeared into the crowd (breaking the woman's heart), ephemeral, with that sheepish, almost boyish smile.

Not before saying to the woman:

'I'm in lo-ove.'

And V. inquiring: 'Man or woman?'

Across the street, the leaning-back flamingo in the window, under the round corner of the flat roof and darkening sky, makes her think, absurdly, of New Orleans. Where, similarly to this place, long balconies deck the backs of courtyards. V. (incongruously) sees a piece of crumpled paper flying down the sidewalk by a café on The Main before High Art invaded. Full of ordinary crazy people, speaking French and English. Although French definitely in ascendance. Water dripping sometimes through the roof. V. sitting there with S., feeling sated despite the tension due to her (V.'s) saying feminism was the antidote to studded belts. Silence. S., finally, showing she still cared enough to close the gap that had opened up between them by speaking first. Her voice, as usual, flat:

'I don't like *isms*. I'm an artist.'

V. (in purple sweater) brushed back a lock, waiting.

A little drip of water fell beside the table. A gay man sitting near them smiled brightly. Outside, that ball of crumpled paper was lodged against the wall. V. waited, still having the confidence of the middle of a relationship: that is, power. S. again reached out. Her flat voice, rising somewhat on certain syllables to get in a complimentary note (which she only used for courting). Saying something most English-speaking women wouldn't even think of saying to a friend:

'This scarf accent-uates your cheekbones.'

The redhead across the room neatly folds a hanky. Is that really her? She has the same savoir-vivre: looking crisp while everyone else's hot. S. was in her element in summer. Nobody wore a sleeveless dress like her: nipped-in waist, bare brightly-golden shoulders emerging from some bright mid-century print (everything she bought was second-hand). The epitome of the urban woman on a summer sidewalk. (Hot wind blowing). Or stepping in yellow print from a shop into the street's glare, holding tapes of Etta James: *The Blues Don't Care.* The down that grew copiously on her arms (since she started living cleaner) dancing a reflection in the summer light.

'What's up?' V. had asked, gluttonous, embarrassed.

The redhead (in the present bar) says: '*Qu'il fait chaud. J'attend ici le bus pour Ottawa.*' Serene, yet disciplined. Jaw held firmly at an angle so as not to betray the looseness of the flesh. S., also from Ottawa, was skinny . But sometimes, when laughing, her jaw hung a little loose due to drinking beer and brandy (no ice, even in the heat). Otherwise, perfect in every manner. Back so straight the shoulder blades practically disappeared in the scoop-necked summer clothes. Or, the time V. spied her at the *Bains Coloniale* where women went in winter for massage and Turkish bath: impeccable woollen underwear. Long straight neck. S. hated sloppiness of any sort. She feared (being bilingual from growing up in the English-dominant capitol) that speaking English caused slackening of the mouth. French being in every way clearer, more precise. Was it the transparency of French (which English pretends to have, but doesn't) that made her keep her life so secret?

V. blinks again. Seeing another ball of paper blow down a sidewalk — in New Orleans. (The association could be the heat). Her eye narrows, reminiscing: not of New Orleans.

But of bygone cafés along The Main where patrons (before the phonier, safer decadence of gentrification set in) were struck by the beauty of S.'s personae. Banal yet mysterious. Worn like masks against the obscure architecture of a summer night.

V. gets an image: S. sitting on some outside steps. With red lips slightly smiling, striped top, nipped-in waist. Like the female lead in a French 50s film. Hanging on (albeit straightbacked) obsequiously to a small, wired poet. Fawning over him as if she cared. From within the dim building that backed the set, synthesizers blasting. To which a male performer in black pants, white shirt, chin angled like a slide rule, moved across a stage cutting the contracted, geometric figures of the 80s. A show called *Business*. 'It's fabulous,' said S. 'I'm totally disillusioned.' Because she could never reproduce, with her spare-yet-softer female body, those angles in a performance of her own. V. (silently) reproached her for wanting to. Tired of her charades: S. reduced everything to theatre. Refusing to use political discernment regarding images. Invoking goddesses instead of sisters . . .

True, she understood the effectiveness of certain art before the critics did.

Also, S. was perfect as Pierrot. Showing up in stripes for a performance called *Dys-sexion*. Building obelisks on stage, from found materials, to use for fucking. (On a video screen an endless stream of female ejaculation.) But every time Pierrot mounted one, legs apart, like a woman, the construction tumbled. Leaving Pierrot in a pile of debris smiling sheepishly. Slowly stripping to become a woman dressed in sequinned green. Fingerless matching gloves. Standing on a grey and white sidewalk in Paris. Then half-nude (although she conspired never to show her breasts) circling the room. On the video screen the body represented as androgynous, bilingual: two halves placed atop a cross. S. coming down the aisle with the rare, love-me smile creeping up her face. Brightening the skin, the dimples, the mischief in the eyes. V. looks across the bar in search of similarities:

The redhead's coolly reading. As if not even waiting for her small, Oriental-looking but Caucasian lover to come back again. V. notes how she now presents herself as pale, light, airy, compared to the bright, outrageously-coloured images of her past. As if to weed out chaos: the pale exterior perhaps permitting a smoother flow of energy. Neither walled up nor leaking wildly out. Yet this self so airy, a touch might make it fly away. The surface of a story (or stories) that wind deeper in the silence. Like that ball of crumpled paper blowing on the sidewalk. Opening it, you'd get some traces of her — if you could catch it.

V. looks out the window at the pediments along the street: garlands, beavers, the fleurs-de-lys. Sometimes (in the past) S. would appear calm, like the redhead. Entering the bar dressed up as guru. V. could *really* drink this in: S. as nurturer. Hair combed back. In loose white clothes after Yoga lessons in the Cooper building. Total fasting was her means of metamorphosis (for the long trip back from junk). V. imagines a room on rue Mentana. A pink dawn roof on which a woman's rolled in a blanket. Watching the brightening of the gas station down below, the park. The skyscrapers of the city. Getting up to work (the day she stopped?). Did an explosion of the mind precede the trip to empty normalcy? The therapies, the exercise, ointments, purges. Even exorcism. Nobody knew as much about the body. So that at a New Year's party (right at the beginning), when V. suddenly went pale and started shivering, S. jumped up and made her Miso soup. It worked. But later, when V. grew round, her purple clothes straining, her dirty-blonde hair limp and hanging in her face, S. refused to aid her in self-improvement:

'There's no point. Un-til you dry up.'

She overdid the therapies, V. thinks, ironically. Nobody did as many. Until so focused on The Self, she was no longer a moving part of the foreground in the street. But, (across the bar, the redhead rolls her hanky) a fixed point of light that can't see past her boundaries. Having even given up the notion of previous incarnations. On this point, V. finds the redhead's mandarin allure (perhaps recalling a dead Chinese ancestor) somewhat reassuring. Because, although, she, V., was anti-esoteric, she found it interesting at least as the basis of discussion that S. (in the past) believed she carried her earlier lives with her. 'What's nostalgic is reactionary,' V. had said to S. But she never managed to get S. cornered in any dialogue about these issues. Attempts at deeper conversation only made S.'s turquoise gaze shift restlessly, non-committally. Carefully drawing energy from the air as if only the energy of the moment could hold the fragmented self together.

V. smiles vaguely. Those fragments S. always projected on the surface covered something else: she and S. went deeper. Meeting often in that dilapidated café (especially during the middle of their relationship), they were almost getting personal. S. talking about a move. To rid herself of lovers: small wired poets who liked to solicit boys in the park. She called them her obsessions. S. was always moving. Sitting on the front steps in the sun. While boxes, carried by her fans, full of throws, shawls, pillows, records, pass and are loaded in a truck. Anyway, after not seeing each other for quite a while, S. took off her coat in the dilapidated, café, to show a black turtleneck, a waist so tiny in its wide belt, that V. held her breath, fearing she was starving. S. said, her flat voice registering below the café's tinkling jazz:

'When I don't have lo-ove, I'm so unhappy. I literally don't know where to put my bo-dy. *Mais quand j'en ai, c'est insup-portable.*'

V. had felt a tightening of the throat. Pausing, after that, in the treed street outside S.'s latest flat and leaning on her bicycle. Looking up at curtains with blood-red birds blowing in the purple frame of the window. Wondering what she wore. Maybe a loose black top and crushed-velvet tights. Pulled on for breakfast following anguished waiting hours in a nightroom trimmed indigo. Paint was peeling off an outside door. Finally, love at dawn, with pink sun rising over tree tops, flat roofs, telephone wires outside the window. And the other (no one could say who) disappeared. S. sat at a table. Drinking a certain tea to eliminate the excesses of the night before. She had to.

S. had also appeared (once) as lesbian. This was the nearest V. got to intimacy with her: a car driving to the country. V. beside her, taking in that odour of herbal bath salts she found maddeningly seductive. Inching closer. S. dressed uncharacteristically simply: black pedal pushers and sleeveless white shirt. A dangling daisy earring. (That French-sporty way of dressing V. noticed on two girls dancing in a riverside bar in 1969.) Then standing on a brilliant summer beach in a faded leotard-for-bathing-suit. Staring at the thick hair growing on her legs: '*Je fais des progrès en tant que lesbienne.* I'm lear-ning not to shave.' A mocking sadness emanating from her golden body. Her lover (not V. who only watched) threw a rubber raft upon the waves. Then ruffle, ruffle over water. Two women in a raft and their legs touch and fingers. Twinkling. Twinkling. Shoreward. Two women with a raft coming up the sand. Small waves, damp feet, a blue sky like her beautiful lover's eyes. S. happy, yet also sad. Although the women's fingers still touched putting the raft of rubber in the trunk. And the blue car and the raft of rubber were going down the road. (V. watching from the back.) And beautiful Etta James, deep blues voice of desire, flooding up the car. Outside the golden dusk, muted beautifully in grey, streaks off the mountains. Then the car stops at wooden steps pattering down to water. Another lake: now in darkness, so a threatening pool. S.'s voice quivering in the night:

'*Eh, les girls, il faut ren-trer.* Unless we're going to New Or-leans.'

V. surveys (more critically) the building across the street. Its flattopped wide-skied air of New Orleans. A place (like Montréal) attracting people who've failed to be a hit in their own language. But in the hot faded dusk, the building's tacky: old slightly crooked aluminum windows, behind which a strip of fluorescent lighting. The pockmarked stone front, the tattered awning, the old signs covering the window of the second floor. In New Orleans (V. in love and losing), the front façades were cleaner, more classic French, being from an earlier period. The wrought-iron balconies on the backs of buildings circling in tiers, even more like Mississippi paddle boats than balconies here. V., sitting in the hotel garden, looked up and saw hardedged clouds over flat flat rooftops. As in a stageset. So hot, she was glad the rooms were dark. The hotel proprietress behind her big fan in the fern-filled lobby. Saying slowly, the better to keep cool: 'y'all c'ld have a-ny room you wanted,' (V. was travelling with a man).

All of them were empty! But the beds were huge and damp. Covered with darkly-patterned spreads and worn rugs: perhaps a former brothel. V. and her partner sank into one, fucking deeply (ignoring the dangers inherent in the lesions on the penis). The jazz floating sweetly on the hot night air.

He the much-desired one and she, so thin in the cavity of her chest. Hunched over listening to the silence grow between them. Later, in a bar, despite the magnificence of her curls, her thin back showed anguish at being able only to raise conversation on the failing merits of the couple. Which didn't prevent her from noticing a Cajun woman speak authoritatively in French to the waiter (whether he understood or not). While her man hung behind. Outside, a crumpled ball of paper rolling down the sidewalk. By which a licence plate lamented: *Ici personne ne parle français*.

Back in Montréal (the man withdrawing), V. naturally called S. immediately. They went and sat in that dilapidated café. As S. took off her coat, V. held her breath. Noting the extreme thinness of S.'s waist and wondering: was it speaking mostly English when she was French that made S. closed yet vulnerable? Always tracing a crooked line from the French-thinking body to the English-speaking words. Strange, S. placed the emphasis on English when she didn't have to. 'It's all theatre, darling,' said the gay man at the next table to no one in particular. Brushing back her lock, V. said (this time kindly) that, REALLY: feminism would help S. synthesize her differences. So she wouldn't be a victim.

'What makes you think I am?' S. said coldly. 'You're the vic-tim: always trying to mo-ther.'

Across the street, the door leading to her place (and the sign shop under it) swings slightly open. The sign-shop men, dressed in white, march past again. The problem being how to fix their sign, which says *Enseignes Simon*, in conformity with the new French-only sign law, over the old one, which says *Simon's Signs* in English, Arabic, Hebrew. Given the new one's inadequate in size to cover the Arabic script, the Hebrew lettering, plus of course the English (writ large) of the old. A huge crash makes V. turn her head.

Simon, the sign-shop owner, has dropped his plate. While changing tables the better to see the operation. Simon says:

'I'm sha-king.' The waitress (not French) brings another, leaning over kindly. He doesn't touch it: only drinks more and more. Shaking violently. V. thinks: 'Clearly a liver problem: angry bile.' So how does he still his hand to paint the big white letters with rounded corners on the bright red signboards in his shop? Simon says:

'Delir-ium tre-mens. Or else nerves from this French ON-LY law.'

V.'s eyelids flutter, exhausted in the heat. Disgusted with Simon's lack of understanding that language needs power to survive. Noting vaguely that the pink flamingo in the third-floor window across the street seems to have changed direction. Leaning back. Conjuring, with its pink tail feathers jutting to the left, a woman in a fuchsia summer dress. All elastic. On a corner, one feathered hip jutting out. If over thirty-five, only a woman eating rice exclusively could dress like that. S. ate rice. Her philosophy in clothes was similar: no additives, no rayon, polyester. Only silk, cotton, wool, excellently maintained. Nobody knew like her how to coax in shape what she skimmed from bazaars and garbage cans. To make tomorrow's fashions. (Except that horrid négligée with fur trim she found behind the fish store.)

V.'s. eyes open — distracted by a low sunray from the street piercing the bar window. Cruelly casting light on the puffiness of the redhead's face. A face that was once so gaunt! Unless it isn't her. For this woman's so serene. But how did she get healed from the restlessness, the emptiness? By living with that Oriental-looking, but, in reality, Caucasian man? With a thumb the redhead smooths her brow. V. notes (almost with satisfaction) that this effort to repress the chaos, to achieve a smooth untroubled surface, may have spoiled her black humour: S. coming down the aisle in clown's colours, balancing on one foot. Half sheepish. Then suddenly sticking out the leg to face you. In striped leotards, as if to say:

Keep your dis-tance.

V. knew the need for distance. Having been, herself, one of those people you meet travelling. Who feel better in another language. Spending hours in her room (in Menton, France) dressing up to pass for French. Perfect hair, little sweater, earrings to match her skirt, fabric shoes. People accused her of remoteness. Except, when lonely or wanting something badly —

'You mo-ther to control. Also, you're chasing me.' S. had added that time in the dilapidated café. V. was stunned. A 'mo-ther' — when she (V.) was radical and cool! (Silently) she mocked S. for being superficial: spending more time on bodily improvements (massages, therapy, creams) when preparing a performance, than on content. So the performance was a piling up of images lacking social context. To make a point about her empathy with people on the street (her own capacity for political analysis), V. gestured out the window. At a kid eating rabidly from a garbage can outside. S. shrugged. *(You're robbed. Her indifference [the junkie connection]. But it doesn't frighten you.)* Shrugging as if V. were waxing sentimental. As if to say: so what? He's probably into spending whatever he rips off on something else. To deflect, V. had focused on the flat voice coming from the cavity of S.'s chest. Clearly, she needed love, nurturing. What irony, thought V. Considering that in the first place (the beginning of the relationship), nurturing was what she, V., had hoped to get from S.!

Across the street, the door to the wooden stairs blows back again. Maybe those stairs do not belong to her. Because who would have turned the pink flamingo round so now its neck is in the foliage and its tail dipping backwards over the planter's edge? Instead of the neck reaching delicately outward as it did before? Given *she*'s sitting there in the bar? And doesn't seem to care the Caucasian Oriental-looking man's gone down the street and hasn't come back again. It could be one of her charades: S. standing with a hatbox on the sidewalk. Or, S. rolling her towel on the burned grass in the park (as neatly obsessive as the redhead just rolled her hanky). The white clouds in the sky making her fear rain. Saying, in a voice made even more dramatic by the flatness and the heat, that a lover tried to cross her courtyard and break a window. Then smiling with worldly understanding. Pulling on her little dress, her turquoise eyes gazing meditatively in the distance. Saying (V. makes an effort to remember):

'The cop was kind of sympa-thetic.'

Surely there was more.

'The God-dess will protect me.'

V. feels the sweat increasing around her neck. Somehow she'd imagined the dialogue between them more significant: S.'s words (especially) floating theatrically across summer nights. Speaking of art and life. Her flat voice dominating the dilapidated café (for those who cared to listen) where they always met (at the middle and near the end of their relationship). Or, at the Schubert Baths which they used for swimming. With tiny black and white tiles, blue and white trim, open showers. V., waiting for S. to rub down with special creams from the healthfood store (unctions, ointments, herbs distilled for use on hair, around the eyes, the heels). Finally saying (grant it, maybe leaning over toward her a little heftily): 'I haven't seen you for a while.' And S. replying, head down (concentrating on the task) voice expressionless:

'Voyons donc, il faut cir-culer un peu.'

In the hot air of the bar, V. feels contradictory desires for ice cream and steamy coffee. She hesitates, looking out the window. The signshop men are on the ladder. But no matter what the angle, the French-only version fails to cover the larger English-Hebrew-Arabic scripts showing underneath. In a lull between the music, the redhead (speaking French) mentions 'Ottawa' again. Swinging her gaze, sea-coloured, even more limpid than before, under thick brows (formerly plucked so thin you could hardly seen them), to look directly forward. The shoulders under her sleeveless blouse evoking summer travelling: a bus, the play of radios, the smell of gum. The bus station in Ottawa. The dusty road to the village (near Ottawa, in the neighbouring English-speaking province) where V.'s grandmother had a house.

But could S. really be from there? She never spoke of origins. Her stiff but elegant stance only showing more confidence than French women who grew up in English-dominant places. Those girls dancing (prudently) by the Ottawa River in a bar. V. knew them well, was always drawn to them. Frances (Françoise) Deguire standing round-shouldered on a village corner (in bright blue air and yellow daffodils). Saying, 'We just broke up.' Meaning her and Stacy, her effeminate Irish trucker lover. V. could sense the panic in her voice. Although Frances (Françoise) was so tough she never cried: just kept everything inside her skinny boy's body. So when V.'s grandmother said not to play with Frances (Françoise) any more, Frances (Françoise) only said: 'Why?' and V., trying make the blow less personal, said, 'Because I'm not allowed on the Back Street where you live.' Seeing all the same how Frances (Françoise) could not shield the pain flickering over her green gaze, her face of an ash blonde.

S. knew how to be more arrogant. Opting to mock the English in the restaurants of Montréal by speaking their language perfectly. At the same time, her Frenchness was a lure. Her chin on one clasped knee in some café, silk scarf tied perfectly around her neck. (How did she achieve creaminess of skin beneath the hairline?) Telling them the anecdotes they loved. Stories of excess. The cousin who died skydiving in a bikini, over Albany. The aunt in Ottawa who'd nearly caused a government to fall, due to a Parliamentarian lover's indiscretion. The voyeurs sitting round her, pale, thin *arrivistes* from English-speaking provinces, suspected her of tactics of diversion. Wanting to penetrate her mysteries. Couldn't she be more personal? Oddly, V. herself had never thought to come out and ask even obvious things directly: Why, in the new Québec where French came first, did S. speak mostly English?

As if in . . . New Orleans.

On the third floor building across the street, has not the pink flamingo changed its stance again? This time leaning sideways. V., grown slightly bleary, due to focusing on a subject so . . . ephemeral. To regain equilibrium she orders cake with icing (like her mother used to make). Wondering why she only comes up with images? Images casting shadows on things like the sparks that passed between them even in the banality of certain conversations. On certain memories: how S. loved her mother, who (S. claimed) had been a crashed pilot in another incarnation. (V. had seen this woman with wild, sky-filled eyes). S.'s generosity towards woman artists. Her sense of excellence. Going up to women at public conferences, and praising their work with exactly the phrase that moved.

'Ton texte m'a fait trem-bler . . .'

Discreetly, V. orders another beer. Thinking how language is inadequate to synthesize her essence. The redhead's still there. Damn, she's asking for the bill. She'll have to think faster: even in a roommate situation (that hot day in the park when S., with her hatbox, asked to come and stay), V. had gained no knowledge of her. Despite carefully watching S.'s precise movements in the hot kitchen of her (V.'s) apartment. S. sitting in her (V.'s) chair working at her (V.'s) typewriter. V.'s cat sitting there beside her. The phone was off the cradle. Maybe S. was never intimate with anyone (in *English* — later V. learned S.'s only true friend was a loyal Gemini as bilingual as her). Coming close, but just when you wanted to get some reassurance regarding the security of the relationship, S. evaded your control. V. suddenly remembers that S. wrote her twice to apologize after things got bad between them. But she (V.) never answered. Just drifted slowly back as if nothing happened. (She hated confrontation.)

V.'s eye closes to cover the transgression. To hide the truth about herself: her terrible romanticism. Preferring bits and pieces of images from the past, tattered flashes of S. separated by a blackness both difficult to grasp and deliciously mysterious — to this pale calm image sitting in the bar. Which has made of carefulness, of security, a science. Unless this excessive carefulness is only another layer: S. sitting in the dilapidated café, her hennaed hair sticking up in a cowlick. Her white face twisting slightly as she lined up the contradictions between balance and objective chance. Saying she refused all but invitations from the marvellous in terms of ordering time. Or, the rich voice over the phone saying: Oh, my cat is eat-ing me. Or the almost titillating fear of the ex-lover trying again to break her windows. Standing up all night checking for fresh footprints in the snow across her courtyard — which was how he came before. V. intervening, she hoped, non-offensively (it being near the end of the relationship). To say maybe loving women was more satisfying. S. replying (ironically?):

'Yeah, more and more are do-ing it.'

Outside, the crumpled ball of paper rolling down the sidewalk.

From her corner, V. sees the redhead standing up. Her clean light form stretching lazily in the air of the noisy, smoky bar. Could that be a stretch of happiness? The loose pants have fallen perfectly around her tiny legs: not a stain; not a wrinkle. V. doesn't have to move any closer to sense the sweet odour of the skin. Redolent of those bathsalts bigger on freshness than on perfume V. never knew the name of. S. was always impeccable to a degree that was astounding, considering her poverty, her depressions. Now the redhead's on the street. Is that S. pattering up the stairs? Maybe to get her suitcase? Or walking (her mother's daughter) towards the sky? Dressed lightly, simply, as if airy enough to fly.

Across the street the pink flamingo in the plantbox has turned again. Now leaning back over the edge so far one of its wire legs is sticking in the air. V. shifts around the hot-yet-air-conditioned breezy table-crowded room. Regretting (she can't help it) what there had been in S. of New Orleans. The polyglot in her, at the table in the dilapidated bar. Where they sat in silence, almost, looking at the crumpled-up piece of paper outside the window lodged against the wall. S. suddenly getting up and running out. V. craning her neck to see the reason why: a taxi at the red light on the corner. Craning harder, V. could see a woman with short hair, small triangular face looking out the taxi's back window. Perfect creamy neck. S. running after it. (Was there a snow-bank?) Screaming as the taxi drove away:

'I love you, you bitch.'

LESLIE DICK'S first novel, *Without Falling*, was published in London by Serpent's Tail in 1987, and in the USA in 1988. Her second novel, *Kicking*, will be published in 1992. She also writes short stories, weird history and, occasionally, art criticism.

ZOË FAIRBAIRNS was born in 1948 and started writing four years later. Her published novels include *Benefits* (Virago), *Stand We At Last* (Virago), *Here Today* (Mandarin), *Closing* (Methuen), and *Daddy's Girls* (Methuen). She has contributed short stories to anthologies including *The Seven Deadly Sins*, *The Seven Cardinal Virtues* (both Serpent's Tail) and *Despatches From the Frontiers of the Female Mind* (Women's Press).

ALISON FELL is a Scottish poet and novelist who lives and works in London. She has published four novels, the most recent of which is *Mer de Glace* (Methuen 1991), and the poetry collections *Kisses for Mayakovsky* and *The Crystal Owl*. Her poetry has been widely anthologised, and she has published essays and stories in collections including *Truth, Dare or Promise*, *Close Company*, *Winter's Tales* and *Whose City?* (Penguin 1991) She edited and contributed to *The Seven Deadly Sins* and its sister volume *The Seven Cardinal Virtues* (Serpent's Tail 1988 and 1990).

MARSHA ROWE is married, with one daughter, and lives in London. She has edited three anthologies for Serpent's Tail, *Sex and the City* (1989), *So Very English* (1991) and *Sacred Space* (1992). Some of her stories/essays have appeared in *Very Heaven* (edited by Sara Maitland), *Stepping Out* (edited by Ann Oosthuisen), *Notebooks, Memoirs, Archives* (edited by Jenny Taylor).

GAIL SCOTT was a journalist for several years, writing about Québec culture and politics for major Canadian newspapers. *Spare Parts*, a collection of short stories, appeared at Coach House Press (Toronto, 1982); *Heroine*, a novel (Coach House, 1987), and *Spaces Like Stairs*, essays at Women's Press (Toronto, 1989). She is also co-author of *La théorie, un dimanche*, (Les Editions du remue-ménage, Montréal, 1988).

LYNNE TILLMAN is the author of *Haunted Houses* (1987), *Absence Makes the Heart* (1990), and *Motion Sickness* (1991). She co-directed and wrote the independent feature film *Committed* (1984). Her essays and fiction appear regularly in *Art in America*, *Bomb*, and the *Village Voice*. Her work has been anthologised in *The New Gothic, Disorderly Conduct (The VLS Reader), High Risk, Top Top Stories, So Very English, Wild History, Between C & D, Blasted Allegories,* and *Sex and the City*. She lives in New York City.

NICOLE WARD JOUVE was born and bred in Provence but has lived her adult life in Britain. Her past: troubled and blessed. Her future: uncertain. She tends to write fiction/autobiography/family history in French, and essays in English, but this pattern is evidently changing. She is the author of *Shades of Grey* (Virago, first published as *Le Spectre du Gris*); *The Streetcleaner: The Yorkshire Ripper on Trial* (Marion Boyars); *Baudelaire: A Fire to Conquer Darkness* (Macmillan); *Colette* (Harvester Press);

White Woman Speaks with Forked Tongue (Routledge) and the novel *L'Entremise* (Editions des Femmes).

MARINA WARNER was born in London of an Italian mother and an English father, and educated at Catholic convents and Lady Margaret Hall, Oxford. Her third novel, *The Lost Father* (1988), was the Regional Winner of the Commonwealth Writers' Prize, 1989. She also writes history and criticism, focusing mainly on female symbolism (*Alone of All Her Sex: the myth and the cult of the Virgin Mary* (1976)). The Erasmus University of Rotterdam recently appointed her to the Tinbergen Chair, where she has been researching fairytale as a medium of women's experience. A new novel will appear in 1992.